HEARTBOUND

P. I. ALLTRAINE

SOUL MATE PUBLISHING

New York

HEARTBOUND

Copyright©2015

P. I. ALLTRAINE

Cover Design by Melody A. Pond

Published in the United States of America by
Soul Mate Publishing
P.O. Box 24
Macedon, New York, 14502

ISBN: 978-1-68291-104-4

ebook ISBN: 978-1-61935-875-1

www.SoulMatePublishing.com

The publisher does not have any control over and does not assume any responsibility for author or third-party websites or their content.

For my husband (Chris),

my parents (Cristina and Frederick),

and my brother (Joren)—my cheering squad.

You allow me to be a writer even when I'm not typing.

Acknowledgements

Creating a fantasy world is easy if there are enough extraordinary people that make reality magical. My husband, Chris—friend, rock, superman, comedian, therapist, magician, genius, and fixer of things—I know you think all my best ideas come from you. You're right. My dearest mother, Cristina, you've been telling me I can be anything, even a writer, for as long as I can remember. Remind me remind me to listen to you more often. My father, Frederick, your wisdom is everything to me, and your sharp eyes when you read my drafts. My brother, Joren, who never reads but reads my drafts, I promise to finish the story you've been waiting for.

Sean, Lohan, Nathan, Zoe, Alyssa, Lance, Naiumie, Syvonne, Lilly, and Caster–never ever stop dreaming, and believing in magic. Felix, Teresita, Eric, Rex, Evelyn, Lolita, Emma, Ike, Luzvil, Merlinda, Hannah, Janea, Nadine, Richmond, Ron, Rexielyn, JB, Roui, Jen, Nathalie, Marc, Joan, Maybelle, Heidi, Jay-R, Franz, Jacob, Angel, Romeo, Cloy, Melanie, Jo, Glenn, Sheree, Richard, Cherry, Shirley, Allen, John, Graham, Mark, and Zoe–there are pieces of you in my writing, and in my heart.

To my Editor, Debby, you made a dream come true. You've given me the liberty to call myself a novelist whenever I feel like it.

I. STRANGER

I defied my fate the moment I leapt out of my apartment's third-story window. I landed on the pavement without a sound. In the same instant, my feet blended into the measured pace in which humans carried themselves.

Gazing up at the sky, I tried to find something to remind me of my home, of my duty. *The future leader of a realm in peril cannot be overcome by irrational desires*, I thought.

Thick smoke obscured the heavens so much even the brightest stars were dull and barely visible. A reminder I was trapped in this city, in this realm. Too far away from everything I knew, too restrained, too human.

Through the chaos in my mind, I captured the image of the girl with brown and dark-auburn tones in her hair, the shine that bounced from her loose curls, the depth in her hazel eyes, and even the awkward half-smile when she caught me looking at her. But the memory wasn't enough. I needed to see her again.

I kept walking until I reached the riverbank in the heart of London. The water rippled with a disheveled mesh of gold and red, reflecting a large architectural structure. My gaze lingered on the clock tower adjacent to the building, gauging its height. A temptation to feel even a fraction of my true nature became a need in every fiber in my body. No longer able to rationalize, my muscles coiled, and I let go. Wind enveloped me with its familiar warmth as I sprang across the River Thames. I aimed to land on the lower portion of the tower, to indulge in the pleasure of my ascent. Though too fast for human eyes, each maneuver, each somersault, each back flip was slow enough for me to savor every moment of my liberation.

On a part of the roof concealed from the passersby below, I was closer to the heavens than I'd been since arriving in the city. Still, I didn't belong here. Hundreds of lights sparkled below me, each representing a life I didn't comprehend. Allowing myself to break free from my human façade had made me a liability to the others. For a few moments of freedom, I let myself forget the importance of my purpose here—the lives that depended on it.

Somehow, having the girl's image in my mind brought calmness within me. One that felt permanent. One that extinguished the sense of entrapment, despite the thick layer of smoke that was still very visible to me. I held on to the calmness as I regained the confidence to face the others.

Since space was a valued necessity of our kind, changes to the apartment's structure had been necessary. The walls and ceilings dividing the rooms and floors of the house had all been removed. As I entered, my attention immediately fixed on Nero, the one most likely to detect my *trouble*. Nero and I shared similar shades of green in our eyes and the warm tones of brown in our hair, but our similarities were not limited to physical attributes. We came from the same Corta, which meant we both had strong connection with the wind and a thirst for knowledge.

Nero, absorbed in yet another book about child psychology, sat on the sofa near a bay window. He worked as a teaching assistant in a primary school, gaining a better understanding of the younger humans. Without moving his eyes from the page, he raised a hand and gave me a quick wave. I noted that he'd read a third of the book, which meant I had at least five minutes to compose myself.

"You're late." I heard Kara's stern voice from the other side of the sofa, surrounded by shopping bags. There was neither a crease on her green satin dress, nor a strand of her flaxen hair out of place.

"I had things to do. I'm an eighteen-year-old university student. I have to play my part well," I said, maintaining a casual tone.

"Things to do." She uttered my words in her usual detached tone. "Do you mean bore your supposedly complex mind with trivial human nonsense?" she asked, without taking her deep-blue eyes off a book on Architectural Photography she'd picked up from one of the shopping bags. I ignored her question and made my way to the other sofa, closer to Dru who was using the cycling machine.

"Hey Pete. Look, I want to show you something." Dru reached for the television remote and flipped from one channel to another. His eyes, almost as dark as his tousled hair, fixed on the screen. It didn't take long before he pressed the buttons harder than necessary. He shook his free hand as though it would speed up the channel change. "Did you know humans organized events just for running?"

"Do you mean the marathons?"

"Yes, I saw it on this earlier," he said, throwing a single nod toward the television. "I think it could be something for me to do, you know—"

"Bad idea," Kara interjected.

"I don't hear any ideas from you."

"It's not my problem," she said with an indifference that provoked Dru's defensive aggression.

"How can you act like you know everything when you're barely doing anything for this mission? Going to museums and shopping is not what we're supposed to do."

"Studying the humans is an integral part of our mission. There is enough to learn from their material creations without having to degrade our existence by attempting to be like them." There was no conceit in Kara's voice as she expressed her approach to our task.

"Our orders were clear. Integrate ourselves into the human realm and understand the humans enough to figure out a way to"—Dru hesitated for a moment—"resist their effect on us."

Kara fell silent. We all did. Not because Dru was right about the terms of our mission, but because we were reminded of the fatal affliction that forced our leaders, our Supreme Eltors, to send us here.

Though we had always been aware of their existence, we had never found it necessary to consider the humans as anything more than distant, inferior beings. Until now. They remained oblivious to our realm, but they were no longer inferior. Within them, they possessed the only element in all the worlds strong enough to kill our Exir, the immortal spirit that dwelled within us. The element was irresistible to us. To consume it would be an act of despicable weakness. It was *Forbidden*.

"With such weak mind, it's a wonder why you find it difficult to adapt to this realm," Kara finally responded. Her words were aimed to move the conversation away from the subject we all avoided, but Dru's tightened lips told me he felt the insult. He was the only one who had yet to find his place in this world. Acting like a human meant he would have to restrain his physical movements. Sitting in a classroom for hours, or doing the same job over and over again wasn't something he could physically tolerate. He'd been spending his days walking and cycling around London, observing as much as he could while moving.

"I think you're going to find it more frustrating," I said, trying to get his attention back before he could launch into an argument with Kara. "Humans can't run very fast. In marathons, they run even slower to save their energy. Even just twenty miles is a fairly long distance for them."

He sighed. "I'm back to doing nothing then."

"We'll find something," I said, attempting to encourage him, though I had no suggestions. I couldn't focus on making him feel better about his situation. I had my own distraction to struggle with. Before I could stop it, the girl's radiant image filled the forefront of my mind.

"Petyr, what's wrong?" Nero asked, interrupting my reverie.

"Why do you ask?" I held my voice with all the calmness I could muster. How would I begin to explain something I didn't understand?

"Something is troubling you," Nero said, careful not to offend me by the obvious implication of his statement.

Dru didn't miss the true meaning behind Nero's cautious words. He jumped from the cycling machine, and in one swift movement, was in front of me. His face filled with urgency as he said, "You're not thinking of the—"

"No," I interrupted to stop him from uttering the word *Forbidden*.

Nero and Dru both looked at Kara, who didn't seem concerned with the conversation. Kara's attention still focused on examining the items in her shopping bags, but there was no doubt she heard our exchange.

"Believe him," she stated after a few moments.

Her detached tone was, for once, music to my ears. Kara's Corta allowed her the ability to discern imminent danger. She offered no more explanation, but it was enough to relieve me from the suspicions.

I was grateful to be released from Nero and Dru's inquisitive eyes. More importantly, I had confirmation I was free to pursue the girl without the danger of falling into the lethal grip of the *Forbidden*. A faint smile inched itself upward on one corner of my lips. This was the first time I was unable to control such minor physical reaction. Dru could have easily seen it if he hadn't already gone back to the cycling machine. Nero had also turned to pick up another book, but I knew he wouldn't be quite as keen to let this go.

"Petyr, are you finding the humans challenging?" Nero asked as he settled back down on the sofa.

No, I thought, *just one—one particularly difficult, strikingly appealing, human.*

"Listen," he continued when I didn't make an attempt to answer, "No one understands your need to figure everything out more than I do. Have patience. We're very new to this realm. You'll find your answers, but it will take time."

"Yes, patience," I agreed, accentuating a grateful tone.

"Don't let your curiosity overpower you," he added.

"I won't," I said with forged sincerity. How I wished it really were just my curiosity. I was used to that. I could handle it better.

I spent the rest of the evening pretending to be interested in Nero's extensive analysis of his students' actions. I supported Dru's attempt and failure to come up with roles he could assume in the human world. I even asked Kara a few questions about the curious human creations she described from her visit to the Tate Modern Museum.

I struggled to keep myself composed. It became especially difficult to disguise a smile whenever the girl's image found its way to the front of my mind. I'd rather not speak, but I knew silence would be more suspicious, so I told them about my day at university, careful not to mention the girl.

When Nero finally announced he was going back to his own apartment, I jumped at the opportunity to leave. "I best get going myself."

"What's your plan for the rest of the night?" Dru asked, a glimmer of hope in his wild eyes.

"I have an essay to hand in tomorrow." The excuse was meant to prevent Dru's interest, but it was a flawed one.

"That will only take minutes. Then what are you going to do, sleep? I'm so bored I could actually sleep!"

I could see he was frustrated, but the idea of him in a state of complete idleness was positively amusing. Though our bodies were capable of sleeping, just like eating human food, we didn't need it. A part of our brain allowed our Nherum form, our physical form, to restore its own energy levels. This meant sleeping would be nothing but a waste of time. Humans should have managed to gain control of this part of the brain. With such short life spans, it didn't make sense they spent half of it unconscious.

"I'd like some time to examine the heavens. The sky seems clear enough." I didn't want to disappoint Dru, but I wouldn't be a good companion for him tonight.

"You all get to connect with your nature, and I can't even go out for a real run without supervision," he protested.

"I'll go with you for a run tomorrow. And I promise to keep my distance."

"Fine," he sighed. The thought of running freely in the woods made his face light up, even for just a second.

As soon as I entered my apartment, I relished my freedom and allowed the girl's image to take precedence in my mind. Much like the shared space, the wall divisions and ceilings had been removed. The only difference was the spiral staircase leading up to a rectangular concrete base, only slightly bigger than a king-sized bed, suspended against the wall. On it was a leather day bed, facing a lunette window. This was where I often settled down during the night.

The other apartments were different from mine. We all had the freedom to tailor our spaces according to our nature. My apartment was similar to the shared house in terms of the white walls and marble flooring, but it wasn't quite as bare. For one, I had a fully functional kitchen as I did intend to cook and consume human food, eventually. I kept everything I needed including a computer desk and a few shelves stocked with books in the four corners of the house, leaving the middle space gratifyingly empty.

Glad to break free from the stringent, slow steps I had to endure all day, I made my way to the staircase. With my right leg forward, the muscles on my left foot pushed my body into the air. I sprang across the room and I landed on the bottom handrail of the staircase, about ten meters from the door. I could have reached the top of the concrete with a single jump, but I ascended with light steps along the spiral metal rail, prolonging the opportunity to move freely as myself. When I reached the top, I allowed myself to fall onto the bed. I placed my hands under my head as if it needed to be supported. My head did feel heavy. There was so much I didn't understand, so many unfamiliar emotions I couldn't begin to explain.

Like Nero, I had initially tried to find the most rational explanation for my increasingly erratic mind. *It must be my curiosity. There's something different about her and I need to figure it out*, I thought. After all, it was in my nature to find answers.

I tried to believe my own justification, but there's one aspect I couldn't explain. I did not simply want to see her again; I wanted her to see *me*. I wanted her to notice me, to pay attention to me. It was an irrational desire, one I'd never experienced before.

II. SERENITY

After sitting through three hours of tedious lectures and a free period, it was time for the one class I shared with the girl. My plan was simple. I wouldn't give her a choice. She would talk to me, and I'd finally understand her.

I was tempted to use my eyes' full capability as I scanned the vicinity. The building structures around the quadrangle blocked my view of the cafeteria, the library, the bookshop, and other places the girl could be walking from. I could easily omit the buildings from my sight and extend my visual perimeter, but I couldn't afford to be reckless again. Besides, Nero had insisted we would have a better chance of understanding the humans if we could see their world the way they did.

When she emerged from the building across the courtyard, surrounded by a crowd of students rushing to their classes, my weak eyes didn't miss her. Seeing her face again *was* better than my memory. Though I expected it, I was still taken aback by how soon the uncharacteristic betrayal of my Nherum form manifested. She had a captivating radiance that seemed to weaken me. My heart had never moved this fast.

"Scarlett," I called when she was close enough to hear me without having to raise my voice. It proved a good decision. I wouldn't have had the strength to speak louder. "Hello," I managed to add when she turned to me. I could see she was unsure if she was looking at the right person.

"Hi," she responded. Doubt didn't leave her expression. Her voice sounded even weaker than mine.

"How was your day?" I was certain this would be an

appropriate opening question, but she seemed to be offended by it. How could I get something that seemed so simple, so wrong?

"What do you want from me?" Her voice didn't carry the resentment I'd have expected from her words, but there was a clear tone of embarrassment. That was when I realized where I went wrong. Most of the students sitting on the benches in the quadrangle, and some who had deliberately stopped walking, were staring at us. Speaking to me had brought her unwanted attention. Her defensive response made complete sense.

"I just wanted to talk to you." I ignored the guilt before it could discourage me from pursuing my intention.

"Why?"

"There's something important I'd like to talk to you about," I pushed, against my better judgment.

"What is it?"

I could tell she was interested, or at least curious to know what I had to say. Either way, it was enough to assure me I could persist with my plan. However, this was no longer the time or the place.

"After class, somewhere more private," I said as I glanced around to point out our conspicuous eavesdroppers.

"Are you asking her out on a date?" asked a feminine voice from a group of girls standing nearby.

I didn't try to find out who it was. I kept my eyes on Scarlett as I went through every human-related piece of information in my brain, searching for the concept of a *date*.

Nothing.

Obviously a date was something of common knowledge. I'd appear suspicious if I were to admit my ignorance. I had to figure this out, a task that would normally be effortless. If only her gaze wasn't so intensely distracting. The girl, who hadn't given me anything more than a few indifferent glances, had her eyes fixed on me. Apprehension crossed her face, but I could see she was interested. A surge of what felt like electric energy shot down my spine. The elated state I suddenly found myself in slowed my brain down. A significant part refused to think about anything other than the wonderful sensation that was very new to me. With much more effort than I had ever needed, I commanded my brain to get to work and recall the recent exchange. I found a statement that could have led to the idea of a date: *somewhere more private.*

"Yes." Despite the distraction, I managed to furnish my answer in good time. "I'd like to ask you for a date."

Scarlett didn't gasp like the others who had been listening to our conversation. She held her breath, and after a couple of heartbeats, she seemed to have forgotten to breathe out. She still bore the same ambiguous expression on her face. I had no idea what it meant. What little confidence I had left crumbled at once.

Had I scared her away so soon after she'd shown the first sign of interest? Had I somehow managed to expose myself to her? I panicked. "Is that all right?" I asked, no longer any sign of confidence in my voice that almost trembled.

She hesitated for one tormenting moment and said, "Okay." Her face reflected the expression I imagined was on mine: a combination of anxiety and relief. I didn't even try to figure out why she would feel the same way I did. We were clearly in opposite positions. For one, she did know what she was saying *yes* to. The important thing was that she'd said *yes*.

The thought of being granted more time with her came with the same wonderful electric sense that seeped through my veins. I smiled at her, hoping she would see how grateful I was. She gave me her usual half-smile, the one she always had when she caught me looking at her. This time, however, the smile wasn't forced. It looked like it was all her tensed figure could manage, but it had warmth that told me she understood my sincerity.

Though I kept my eyes locked onto hers, I could feel each attentive stare from our uninvited spectators. It was selfish to put her through this. I needed to get her away from here. I wanted to, and I would, but her eyes held me, restrained me. I was unable to move until she released me.

"We're late for the lecture." She glanced at her watch, interrupting my warm captivation.

"Shall we?"

She shrugged and entered the building without giving me another glance, like she understood what her eyes could do to me. I strode beside her, but neither of us spoke. I needed the time to recover my confidence. Why was my supposed resilient physical body crumbling after just a brief exchange with her? I was clearly missing something, so I adjusted my auditory range to hear the whispers outside the building. I needed some help to comprehend the intensity that came from something which, in theory, should have required much less effort. I was sure even Nero would agree that finding out what was making me so weak, that my body had to work very hard just to stop my knees from shaking, was a valid reason to use my full hearing ability.

Who the hell was that girl?

I can't believe he just asked some random girl on a date. I mean, she's not ugly or anything, but still, life is so unfair!

She didn't even look excited about the whole thing! He is so wasted on her!

I'm sure I saw the cardigan she was wearing on sale in Topshop, and he's wearing an Armani shirt from the latest collection! They are so not meant to be!

She's definitely not pretty enough, not for him, and not with that hair.

I never thought I'd prefer to have any of my senses at human level, but I could no longer listen to the negative comments about Scarlett. Each insult directed at her instigated a sharp, unpleasant tension around my chest and my forehead. It must be guilt. After all, I was the reason she became the subject of those insults. I should have known better than to rely on humans to help me understand my own emotions. They were inferior, inadequate. This had always been a fact, but I flinched at my own harsh assumptions. A part of me refused to degrade the race that produced the fascinating individual who walked beside me.

I looked at her, searching for what was rapidly changing my mind-set. There was absolutely nothing wrong with her hair. The loose curls perfectly accentuated her effortless beauty. But the others had a point when they said she wasn't pretty. That was far too inferior a word. I struggled to take a deep breath. How beautiful she looked to me was overwhelming.

Several heads turned in our direction when we entered the hall, but the professor didn't let us interrupt his lecture on Lord Byron's *Don Juan*.

"Do you mind if I sit beside you?" I whispered as I followed her to the seats in the back row.

"You can sit wherever you want."

I wanted to be close to her so much that I took her indifference as approval. When I settled into the chair next to hers, I became more aware of my weakened physical state. The tension in my chest strained every breath, and the beads of sweat that trickled down my forehead were juxtaposed with the cold dampness in my palms. I was barely able to regain my strength when the lesson was over. I needed to take a deep breath and a couple of seconds to ensure my legs would be strong enough to lift me off the chair. *I could do this,* I thought to myself as feeble attempt to sustain my confidence. "Where did you park?" I asked Scarlett as I followed her out of the lecture hall.

"I don't drive to Uni," she replied with a slight snicker.

"Why not?" I realized why she would find driving in the city inconvenient, but I asked anyway just to hear her voice again.

"London traffic and crazy parking rates ring any bells?" she said with a smile.

I needed a couple of moments before I could speak again, so I smiled back to buy some time.

"I drive. It's not that bad." I fought a smirk as I thought about how easy it was for me to drive in the city, even with the limited speed. Calculating the changes of the traffic lights, precise lane crossings and tactical maneuvers meant I never had to be caught in the middle of a traffic jam. "Shall we head to my car? We could go somewhere private to talk." I was still not completely sure what a date was, but I knew holding on to the idea of going *somewhere more private* was adequate.

"This doesn't have to be a big thing. You were kind of pressured into saying you wanted to ask me out on a date. I know you just wanted to tell me something, so you can just tell me now."

"Your jumper is too thin."

"What?" she asked, clearly taken aback by my seemingly unrelated response.

"You must be freezing."

"Well, you're not even wearing a jumper," she said, gesturing her right hand to my cobalt-blue cotton shirt.

"I know. I'm freezing," I lied. "We should go somewhere nice and warm. Hot coffee would help, too." I couldn't possibly tell her that the September weather didn't affect my Nherum form, which could warm itself even if it was trapped in a glacier.

"Fine." She shook her head, and a smile appeared on her face. "There's a café across the road from the campus."

I returned her smile and walked with her to the café, cramped with round tables and wooden chairs too close to each other. She chose the table in the corner by the front window, and I headed to the counter. I wanted to make sure she'd have enough to drink during the conversation, so I ordered a large cappuccino and a bottle of water. I also bought some food just in case she was hungry. Humans needed food regularly, and lunch was hours ago.

"You don't expect me to eat all that, do you?"

"Just the ones you like," I replied and sat on the chair across from her. Since I didn't know which ones she would prefer, I decided to get six pastries, one of each type the café had.

"I'm not hungry."

"Not now, but I might keep you a while." I tried to maintain a lighthearted tone to conceal my genuine, outrageously strong, desire to stay in her company.

She sighed as if to brace herself. "Say what you have to say." Her voice was a soft whisper, yet her eyes commanded me.

How could I refuse?

"You never look at me." I didn't care if my statement sounded strange. She'd made me incapable of anything but honesty. In that moment, I knew the problem was far more than just the peculiar way my Nherum form reacted to her. She was a danger to my purpose. I was vulnerable in her presence. She could ask me anything, she could ask me what I was, and I'd have to tell her. I should walk away before I could tell her something she shouldn't know, before I jeopardized my mission.

But maybe she wouldn't ask, I heard a faint voice in my mind say. With one thought, I'd justified my decision to stay. Even if I had the strength to tear my gaze away from her, I wouldn't walk away. I wanted to be here, in this uncomfortable chair, more than anywhere in this realm.

"Excuse me?" she asked in a steady voice, but her uncertainty revealed itself through the slight crease between her eyebrows.

"You don't see me, not like other people do. Everyone shows interest, but not you." I struggled to explain.

"And you're offended by that?" she asked with a humorless laugh.

"No. I'm just trying to figure out why you're so different." I leaned forward on the table, moving my face a few inches closer to hers. I stared deeper into her eyes, desperate for her to see the seriousness in mine.

"I'm not trying to be different." She hesitated for a moment and continued in a softer voice, "I was just being realistic."

"Realistic?" I had no idea what she meant.

"Well, I didn't want to waste time looking at someone who'd never look at me."

I laughed.

"What's so funny?"

"You're much, much more sensible than I am. You see I should've known better, but there I was wasting time, looking at someone who never looked back at me. But the thing is, it didn't feel like a waste of time."

"I don't know what to say to that." She turned and stared outside the window.

"Why?"

"Because you're Petyr-frigging-Crest. We've only been at university two weeks. Most people haven't even memorized their timetables yet, but they know your name. They write it all over their notebooks, with hearts and frigging butterflies. They even know to spell it with a Y instead of an E. Some of them will probably never remember that William Cowper's surname, whose work we've been studying since Week 1 by the way, is spelt with OW and not double O. I'm rambling, I know, because there are girls who actually hang around your classrooms hoping you'll notice them. And you're saying that you're looking at me?" She exhaled a single laugh, and repeated, "Me?"

And thinking about you, like a crazy person. She didn't need to know that, so I simply nodded.

"What do you want from me?" Her expression grew thoughtful once again, but her tone was earnest.

I wanted so much from her. I wanted her to help me understand the erratic and irrational way she made me feel.

I wanted her to tell me why I could hardly breathe. I felt like I was drowning every time I saw her, yet I refused to look away. I wanted her to smile at me. I wanted her to keep me a prisoner of her captivating eyes for a little longer. I wanted her to lean closer to me for reasons I couldn't comprehend. I wanted her to stay here with me even though she made me so dangerously weak. I wanted so much from her, but more than anything, I wanted to know her.

"Will you let me get to know you?"

"You won't find anything interesting." She flashed me a tentative smile that triggered my heartbeat.

"Everything about you is interesting."

She sighed, and my first full conversation with a human followed. It proved unexpectedly easy. We talked about everything, even the most trivial things, from the weather to the cold pastries on our table I had convinced her to try. My heartbeat was still irregular, my hands were still trembling slightly, and I was still powerless every time she locked her eyes on mine. But I felt calm. I think she felt the same. Though my judgment was slightly unreliable, the change in her facial expression was clear. Ease, and even interest, replaced the traces of doubt and apprehension. She seemed oblivious to the considerably darker street on the other side of the window, something I willingly took as confirmation I had her complete attention. The thought was both gratifying and overwhelming.

I wished I were able to lose track of time. Despite my current flawed mental prowess, I knew we had been talking for one hour and forty-seven minutes. I had to let her go.

"Have you got any plans for tonight?" I asked, casually allowing her to think of the time.

"I have to finish reading *Oedipus Rex* for tomorrow, but that's about it."

Maybe she didn't lose track of time at all, maybe she deliberately chose to stay longer than I ever thought she would be willing to.

"Gosh, is that the time?" She lifted her arm to have a closer look at her watch, strapped on her left wrist with worn leather.

"You lost track of time," I heard myself utter.

"I guess I did. I have to get going. I have to finish the book and get some sleep for an early start tomorrow."

"A full day today, then an early start tomorrow? That's hardly fair." I'd normally say humans should make the most of what energy they had and use their limited time wisely. They already wasted so much time sleeping. But I thought of how little energy Scarlett's delicate frame would be able to sustain. I wanted her to rest, to waste as much time as she needed.

"Yeah, the tubes are terrible in morning rush hour. I finish at eleven, though," she explained with a smile that had grown warmer each time. "I have the rest of the day off, so hopefully it won't be so bad."

I noticed that seeing the positive side of an otherwise unfavorable situation was one of her many intriguing traits. By nature, my Corta could instantly see and calculate possible angles of every situation. My methodical mind was too certain, too precise to tolerate anything that was plainly inaccurate. This was why I couldn't share the optimism in her statement, but I couldn't reject her attitude either. In fact, a part of me wished that I, too, could have the strength to ignore the odds and be hopeful. This wasn't possible for someone from my Corta, for someone who knew too much.

Then I realized when it came to Scarlett, I hardly knew anything. No matter how much she told me about herself, I'd always want to know more.

I knew her name.

Scarlett.

The sound of her name reverberated in my mind. She was no longer just a human girl. She was *Scarlett*.

"How about I take you to lunch after your class?" Perhaps I could do something to increase the odds and justify her hope for a good day.

She hesitated for a couple of seconds. "I guess I have nothing much to do after class."

"Is that a yes?" I was hopeful, but not against the odds.

When she uttered the word *yes*, I felt something different. Something that had always been there—lurking underneath the excitement, the fear, the anxiety, the desperate longing to be close to her, and the increasingly unruly physical reactions. Stronger than anything I had ever felt in my centuries of existence, yet it brought a sense of serenity to my conflicted temperament. Despite being plagued by the thoughts and emotions I struggled to explain, I was positive of two things. I needed to know more about Scarlett, and that she made me feel like I had the liberty to do so.

I knew she was perfectly capable of going home by herself, but I felt the need to keep her safe. I offered to drive her, but she laughed and teased that she would get home faster if she hopped backwards the whole way. If I were to drive her, I'd have to do it like a human, and she would be right about how unnecessarily time consuming it would be.

Letting her walk away without knowing for certain if she would reach her destination safely triggered my brain to calculate the risk of accidents and other possible dangers she could easily come across. I had to remind myself this was something she did every day.

When we reached the station, I stood there, knowing I couldn't offer to go with her. Once, Nero convinced me to use the London Underground. When we descended further away from the open air, surrounded by a crowd that moved too close around us, my instincts began to retaliate. Nero had to use a considerable amount of force to pull me into the carriage, swarming with bodies. When the doors finally opened at the next station, Nero knew better than to make an attempt at stopping me from getting out. I'd never know how he could stand it for a full forty minutes twice every day.

I needed almost a full minute to compose myself after Scarlett had disappeared into the underground station. My own disappointment mocked me. I wasn't even strong enough to endure a few minutes of discomfort inside the tube carriage.

I walked to my car and drove to the shared apartment as fast as I could. I wanted to speed through time so I could be with Scarlett again. I knew time wouldn't go faster no matter what I did, but I *hoped* for it to trick me again.

I was glad to see Dru standing outside the apartment as I drove into the street. He was wearing a pair of black gym shorts, a white tank top, and some lightweight trainers. If he didn't constantly move his arms and heels like he was warming up for an evening run, he would've looked underdressed for a drafty autumn evening. Well, he *was* going for an evening run, just not the kind the onlookers, like the woman pushing a child's pram and a man carrying bags of groceries, would assume.

From Dru's impatient expression, I knew I wouldn't need to stop the car. This was a good thing. I needed this run more than he did. I slowed the car down—to speed things up.

As expected, Dru's impatience soon took over. The man with the groceries was visibly taken aback as Dru broke into a sprint and whizzed past him. He glanced at Dru for a brief second, but the heavy bags induced him to carry on walking.

When Dru reached my car, he laid his right palm flat on the hood and swiftly lifted it with his fingers, releasing just enough force to raise his entire body into the air, over the car. Whilst mid-air, he reached for the door with his left hand and landed on the passenger seat.

"You're so reckless," he said in a transparently exasperated tone as he shut the car door with far more force than it needed.

"You leap over my law-abiding moving vehicle, and I'm

reckless?" I said, trying to suppress a smile.

"You knew I wouldn't be able to resist. Someone could have seen. That lady—" He pointed at the woman with the pushchair a few meters behind us. Unlike the man carrying his groceries, the woman would have been facing directly at the car to see Dru's minor stunt. If only she wasn't too busy trying to pull down the plastic cover over the pushchair.

"Yes, I knew you wouldn't be able to resist," I interrupted, "But I also knew the lady wouldn't see you. It started to drizzle just before you moved."

"Too close." He sighed, sounding more relieved than annoyed.

"Too precise." I laughed and added, "And reckless, definitely reckless."

Dru shook his head, but traces of a smile were already visible. He didn't always take the rules too seriously. It was in his Corta's nature to crave the thrill of impulsiveness. I should feel guilty for exploiting his limitation, but I was no longer in a better position than he was. Since I discovered my own weakness, I had taken too many risks. I was more of a liability than he ever would be.

"Why didn't you wait for me inside?" I asked.

"I just had to get out of there."

"Nero was getting unbearably irritating."

"What is it now?"

"It's probably because Kara was very good at ignoring him, so I was the easier target. He kept talking about you, kept asking me to participate in his plan."

I knew what Nero was trying to do. More importantly, I knew where this conversation was going. I slowed the car down to just less than ten miles per hour to ensure we stayed within Nero's hearing range.

"Plan?" I suppressed a grin, anticipating Dru's answer.

"Yes, he asked me to observe you closely. Well, that's how he put it, but really, he wanted me to spy on you. He was trying to teach me what signs to look for and what to report back to him. He said it would be for everyone's benefit, but obviously I refused to do anything behind your back."

Nero's attempt was as pitiful as I had expected. "Shame, you could've caught me off guard." The smirk on Dru's face was confirmation he knew this statement wasn't directed at him. Imagining the look on Nero's face as he listened to his embarrassing failure was acutely satisfying.

"What took you so long anyway?" Dru asked when we'd moved far enough from Nero's prying ears.

I needed a few seconds to think of what to say. Telling him I was on a *date* would require too much explanation. I needed to keep my words short and ambiguous. This was the first time I would talk about something in direct relation to Scarlett. I wasn't sure how long I could hold myself together before Dru noticed anything.

"I got held back," I said carefully.

"Human?"

Dru uttered the one word that made every fiber of my being scream for the image of Scarlett.

Human. Yes, a human was the reason *I got held back*. The reason my foot had involuntarily stomped on the brake pedal. The reason I sat here frozen, with my hands clinging on the steering wheel for actual support. The reason I was rapidly losing control of my physical body.

After what felt like the longest pause I had ever needed to take, I uttered the word, "Yes." The single syllable carried so much weight in emotion. Dru heard it all. I couldn't bear to see my own shock, confusion, fear, and disappointment that were equally visible on his face.

"What?" he managed to whisper after a pause that was longer than mine. It wasn't a question, but rather a plea for an explanation.

"I don't know what to say." It was the truth.

"Is Nero right?" From the building alarm in Dru's voice, I could tell where his thoughts were headed. He was wondering if I had been tempted by the *Forbidden*.

"No," I replied without hesitation. This was the one thing I was sure about.

"But—"

"There is nothing to worry about," I interrupted, so he couldn't entertain the thought further. What was happening to me had nothing to do with the *Forbidden*. I was sure of it. Of course, I was sure of it.

"I've never once seen you like this, and I've known you for a very long time, Pete. You didn't even know what to say, and you're skilled enough to make sure I don't notice that. Something is wrong. We have to tell the others."

"There will be no need." The thought of having everyone see my weakness was excruciating. There would be many questions, and I had no answers to give them right now. I needed more time. I had to convince Dru this was something I could deal with on my own. "It's just a minor setback. I can handle this."

He squinted, like he struggled to confront my words.

He didn't believe me. I kept failing, I thought. I'd failed myself so many times in the last twenty-four hours.

"A minor setback?" he finally said. "Pete, I caught your hesitation. In fact, I saw more than that. I saw emotions you'd never have allowed me to see. It wasn't a minor setback. It was impossible. There's only one thing that could cause you to lose yourself like that, and you know it."

"No, I don't, and neither do you. We barely know anything about humans. This could easily be something else. I had never looked at any human and yearned for the *Forbidden*. You know me better than to think I could ever be so weak."

"You're right. We don't know enough about humans to be sure they have no other effect on us, but this is precisely why I should insist we tell the others. I can see you're going through something that's possibly bigger than you think, but yes, I do know you. I have to trust you and let you handle this on your own for now. For centuries of loyalty, I owe you that much. But you have to be honest with me, about everything."

"Soon," I promised. I'd tell him everything, but for now, we both needed to be somewhere. I pushed my foot on the acceleration pedal until the back wheels screeched, drowning the roar of the engine.

As we approached an undisturbed forest outside the city, Dru jumped out of the car, stripping off his tank top and trainers. He vanished behind the trees before the car came to a full stop. My brain worked faster, but physical speed was on his side. By the time I stood in clearing, he was already deep in the woods. Running after him would be hopeless, but I had another way of catching up.

I moved one leg forward and bent my knees until they were a couple of inches from the ground. Almost instantaneously, my toes coiled and my shoulders flexed to push the rest of my body up into the air. Once off the ground, I was able to match Dru's speed. I shot up higher and higher to the space between the forest and the full moon. Up here, I could see the entire forest and everything in it. The moon was bright enough to illuminate even the tiniest insect crawling on the ground.

Though Dru's speed made him practically invisible to human eyes, I spotted him almost as soon as I looked down. Calculating his speed with mine, I descended to the direction he was heading and landed on the spot he would have been a couple of seconds later. When he saw me standing in his way, he grabbed hold of a branch and swung himself up to the tree next to me.

"I thought you'd never catch up," he said lightheartedly.

"I believe I got here before you," I replied in the same tone.

"I'd like to see you get anywhere before me without cheating." He grunted and moved without giving me a chance to reply. He'd always been convinced that without the help of the wind, I couldn't possibly be physically faster than him. I stood back to let him relish his run and his time with nature. *I could afford to stay behind for a few seconds*, I thought, smiling to myself, knowing I could catch him up whenever I decided.

When I leaped into the air, I didn't bother looking down to find Dru. This time, I focused my attention up above. The sky wasn't much clearer so close to the city. Still, I reveled in having the freedom to jump and experience even a fraction of my old life. Above the forest, cloaked in the wind, I was in full control of myself for the first time since my incident in the city. This time, I was liberated but not reckless. Every jump made me feel stronger, closer to my real self.

Parts of my senses were constantly monitoring Dru. I intended to keep off his tracks. He deserved his freedom to run without the interruption of watchful eyes, but I had to make sure he didn't lose control and run too close to civilization. I jumped to his direction, only throwing quick glances when I was furthest away up in the sky. The higher I was, the clearer I could see. Up here, his skin was more luminous with the moonlight.

In spite of his speed, I could hear each steady heartbeat. I could see each strand of hair that swayed wildly as he circled the forest. I could feel his serenity as he moved with remarkable precision.

Physical contact with nature was the source of his strength and speed, and nature welcomed him with open arms. His movements were spontaneous, his direction constantly changing, but caused no destruction to even a single leaf. The trees guided his way, directing his senses to move his body in the most exact way that wouldn't disturb any life.

Dru was part of a Corta with strong connection with nature. He could hear the trees, read the land, and converse with animals. During his run, he often lingered to communicate with nature. He would cling to tree trunks and swing around branches. When he landed on the ground, he would bend down so his palms rested flat on the soil before springing onto another tree.

Whilst mid-air, I stopped sensing movement from Dru, driving me to swerve to the direction of one moonlit complexion. He was frozen in the midst of a cartwheel, with both palms flat on the ground and legs up in the air. He was staring intently into the land that was merely a couple of inches from his face. He must be reading it.

"What's wrong?" I asked.

"We're not alone."

"Humans?" I uttered in disbelief. We were too far into the forest for humans to be nearby, especially at this time.

"No." His voice was quiet, but I could sense his panic.

"One of us." My voice wasn't as quiet as his, with panic only slightly better concealed.

He finally tore his eyes away from the ground and gave me a single sharp nod and whispered, "Trouble."

III. ENCOUNTER

Trouble. My heels lifted at the sound of the word. Every muscle in my body was primed for a jump.

"He's one of mine," Dru uttered in a disheartened whisper as he got on his feet.

His statement stopped me in my tracks. This meant the cause of trouble would have been aware of our presence in the same way Dru was of his. We had no time to waste. I looked at Dru's face for answers, but found only uncertainty.

"The pain, it's unbearable." Anguish rang in his voice.

Why would this being hurt his own kind, and how could he manage to do it without being seen? No time for answers. We shouldn't have been here long enough to ask the questions.

"We're wasting time, Dru. We have to move." I grabbed both of his arms, ready to lift him up.

"No, we don't," he said in the same distressed tone as he placed one hand on my shoulder to push my heels back down on the ground. Genetically, Dru was considerably stronger than me, so there's no way I could move him if he didn't let me.

"What's wrong with you?" I clung to whatever patience I had left.

"There's no threat to us."

"You're in pain." I almost shouted the words.

"I hear his pain."

He is the one in trouble? "Hearing his pain shouldn't cause you this much distress."

"And what do you think is happening? Do you really believe that our own kind, one who shares my Corta, would attack me? For no reason?" Dru asked, evidently offended by my assumption.

"For reasons I chose not to waste time figuring out while you're in agony."

"Since when did you need time to figure things out? Pete, if it hasn't made sense to you by now, then it just doesn't make sense." Dru attempted to speak lightheartedly. He clearly found the current deficiency in my skills amusing, but a shade of torment remained on his face.

"Good point," I said, trying to return his intended tone. The pain that surrounded him hadn't affected his speed. He was out of my sight as soon as I lifted my heels.

This time, I didn't look up at the heavens as I jumped. I closed my eyes and focused my senses on monitoring Dru. I listened carefully to every heartbeat, to every breath, to every ounce of blood flowing through his veins. I searched for signs that his calmness was being disrupted, for signs of danger. He claimed there was no threat, but the agony on his face didn't allow me to dismiss the possibility easily.

When I sensed him slow down, I landed a few feet ahead to scan the surroundings. The being was tucked in the shadows between the large roots of a tree. He was sitting on the ground, arms folded on his knees to support his head. A blanket matching the shadows covered most of his body. Undoubtedly, this being didn't want to be seen. No sign of movement, apart from the sound of his weak lungs struggling to drag slow shallow breaths. In spite of curiosity, I willed myself to step back. This was Dru's concern. The curiosity Dru bore on his face had far more depth than mine. There was also immense pity in his eyes that wasn't directed to the being. His sight was fixed on the tree the being rested against.

Dru stepped to the tree, but stopped when he was close enough to touch it. He seemed as though he wanted to move closer. His body leaned forward, but his feet were rooted to the ground.

Pausing several times, Dru lifted one arm. With eyes closed, he held his breath as he slowly reached for the trunk with the very tip of his fingers. Dru barely touched it when his mouth fell open and drowned his lungs with air, emitting a violent scream. As if an exceptionally strong force had hit him, his other arm clutched his stomach.

He stared at his fingers that were still touching the tree. Each breath he drew carried a deep, piercing tone of agony. I had to intrude. I pulled his hand from the trunk, and as soon as I let go, he collapsed to the ground. I attempted to help him up, but he was unable to move.

"What's going on, Dru? Let me get you out of here," I urged, grabbing his shoulders to lift him up.

"No! He is my kind, from my Corta. You know I can't leave."

"But what can you do? He hasn't acknowledged our presence. We have to get back and figure out why you're suffering this much," I reasoned with urgency, but it was futile.

"I can't leave him, Pete. I felt his pain. I won't turn my back on him."

"His pain? Look at him, not even a single twitch, nor a single sound. He can't possibly feel even half of the pain I just witnessed you suffer."

"The tree he is in contact with screams of it."

I understood that since they were of the same Corta, they were both one with Nature. Nature could feel them and they could feel Nature. Dru must have heard the cry of the tree that felt the pain of the being leaning against it. When he touched the tree, the pain Dru felt would have been nothing more than a minute portion of the pain that coursed through the silent, motionless being. Only one thing could cause that amount of agony to our kind. I shook my head, wanting to erase the harsh realization.

"There's no other explanation, but it doesn't matter. We have to help him," Dru said as though he read my mind. He tried to lift himself off the ground but only managed to sit up. It seemed the agony that still enveloped his body didn't permit him to go any further.

"You're too weak. I can't let you do this." I refused to risk Dru's safety to save someone who was weak enough to submit to the *Forbidden*.

"I'll be fine. He needs my help." His manner made it clear that, for him, this wasn't a matter of choice.

"Dru—" I tried to protest, but he raised a hand and gestured for me to stop. "We're helping him," he ordered with an even stronger conviction.

"You're not helping anyone," a weak, husky voice interrupted. Distinct authority was surprisingly audible in the trembling whisper.

I turned my attention to the being that had now lifted his head up, but his neck seemed too weak to keep it there. Though his head was slightly tilting up and down, his piercing eyes were fixed on me. I looked away. I couldn't bear to keep my gaze on his distorted face.

"He doesn't have long, Pete, please."

"My friend is willing to help you. He's willing to give you his"—I hesitated to say the word he didn't deserve—"Antidote." I addressed the being with my eyes fixed on the ground.

"Look at me," the frail voice demanded.

I closed my eyes, refusing the sight of his sin.

"Look at me," he repeated. This time, every tremble in his voice accentuated the ambivalence between his plea and his command.

"Stop wasting time!" Dru's voice was thick with anguish.

I rested my gaze on the being's face, focusing on his eyes. The discoloration of his iris from brown to gray, covered by a thick layer of cataract, and the ruptured blood vessels were already more than what I was prepared to witness. When he slowly leaned out of the shadow, the moonlight illuminated every bit of distortion.

I felt a twist in the pit of my stomach as I beheld his decaying face. The skin on his left cheek had disintegrated, exposing his fractured, decomposing cheekbone. His dry, wrinkled lips were covered in pus and crusty blood. What's left of his teeth were rotted black. Parts of the moldering skin on his face were a shade between yellow and black. The rest were thin layers on exposed veins. His hair, the patches that were left, were translucent white.

I held my breath when his frail hands threw off the blanket covering the rest of the dire sight. I exhaled only when I saw he was wearing a T-shirt, relieving me from the sight of his putrid internal organs. The T-shirt hung on his shoulders as it would on a couple of thin poles. His exposed arms had little more than patches of cracked skin, traced by fresh blood.

He was rotting by the second, right in front of my eyes.

"It's not too late," I replied to the stranger. As long as his heart was beating, he could be saved.

"Do you think someone who does this to himself is worth saving?" I could tell he already knew my answer. And he was right, but I couldn't validate his sentiment, not in front of Dru.

"You made a mistake," Dru interrupted. "You can deal with the consequences later, but for now, here, take your antidote." Dru raised his arm toward me as an instruction that he was ready to do what was necessary.

"I won't take the young Arca's blood," the being almost screamed in disgust. He uttered the name of their Corta, Arca, with such detachment as though he no longer considered himself as one. Only the blood of those born to lead our world, the Eltors, could restore someone who had committed the *Forbidden*. Like Dru, I was an Eltor, but the source of the blood had to be from the same Corta as the sinner. This was between him and Dru, yet the being looked at me, addressed me. Perhaps he knew without me, Dru couldn't perform the task that would save his life.

"Alex!" Dru yelled the being's name, which he would have learned from the trees.

"Please, we have no time," I said with less compassion than Dru. Using Dru's blood in his weakened state wouldn't be my verdict, but it was his antidote to give. It wasn't my place to deny him the right to decide.

"It wasn't a mistake. It was a choice. There is nothing to face later. This is the consequence. Look." His hand trembled as he raised his index finger. We watched the brittle skin, where the nail plate used to be, turn into a darker shade of mauve. "You see how fast it's eating its way to my core? That's because I made the choice over and over again."

"Now that you know the pain, you can learn from it." Dru wasn't willing to give up.

"I'd make the choice again if I could. It would be a waste of your precious blood, Eltor," he spat on the last word. "I'd do it again, over and over and over again."

"And put yourself through this again? A fraction of your pain was almost unbearable to me. Why would you? How could you?" Dru should condemn the being's lack of remorse, but he was too confounded. His question sounded more like a plea for enlightenment than reproach.

"Sublimity at its highest, elation no creature in any world can even dream of. How can I regret that?" A faint smile graced his distorted lips when he uttered the words.

"You can recover, forget—"

"That's not going to be possible," Alex interrupted Dru.

"You know you can forget," I insisted.

"I don't want to," he declared in the same weak voice. Without giving me a chance to reply, he continued, "Even if I was willing to forget the glorious sensation, I couldn't possibly carry on. If you had done the *Forbidden*, could you go back home? Could you face them?" He asked the questions slowly with such serenity. It seemed he had already accepted the reality of his situation, and once again, he knew what my answer would be. He stared at me with his clouded eyes, begging for liberation.

"No," I finally managed to whisper. I felt an unexpected sadness at the realization that this being, that I didn't care to save in the first place, never had a chance of being saved.

"Pete!" Dru objected.

"Then let me be." Alex closed his eyes and rested his head back on his folded arms.

"No! Pete, he doesn't know what he's saying. We can't let him die. We can't lose another one." Dru used what energy he had left to lift himself up and run to the withering being. He extended his arm, ready to perform the act himself.

"He's already dead. We can't save him," I said, urging him back.

"He's only got seconds left!"

"There's nothing we can do."

"How can you say that? I'm here, right here! I can save him." Dru struggled to free himself from my grasp, but I was stronger than him right now.

"Let him go, Dru," I said with more authority than I intended.

"No . . . No . . . No!" Dru screamed in both protest and pain.

The last few seconds were supposed to be the most painful. Even more painful than having felt the gradual decomposition of every part, every inch of his skin, every strand of his muscles, every single vein until his entire physical body was dead.

Alex's body was tensed. Each breath seemed more difficult and heavier than the last. He extended his right hand and struggled to lift it. The other clutched his chest tighter. He pointed straight at Dru as he said, "You'll understand. You're very close. Just let go. It's worth every pain." He dropped his hand back on his chest, closed his eyes, and surrendered his body to embrace its brutal destiny.

I was standing behind Dru with my hands on his arms, frozen. So was he. Alex's words were like sharp arrows that went straight through Dru to hit me in the core of my heart.

He was speaking to me. I knew it. Dru knew it.

The words that came out of a wretched sinner made too much sense. Before I could pursue the thought that would condemn me, I was haunted by a shrill sound I didn't expect Alex was still capable of producing.

Death had crept into his heart, the final physical part to die. It was also the hardest to kill. Our hearts kept us alive, beating, for centuries. For the deterioration to penetrate the single most solid part of our Nherum form meant pain far more excruciating than any ordinary human body would be capable of feeling.

But this wasn't the worst part.

The heart would crumble. When it stopped beating, the Nherum would finally reach its death. The physical pain would cease, and the real torment would begin.

In the heart's core laid the Exir, our essence. It's enclosed within a translucent mantle, meant to be impenetrable. From Alex's twisted body and the deafening sound of his torture, this was clearly not the case. Committing the *Forbidden* was the only time death could slither its way through the center of the heart, and bang on the mantle until it cracked and shattered into pieces. It would be inexorable, the kind of agony that no creature would want to know. Ripping the mantle from the Exir would be like slowly peeling its natural skin, but it was so much more than mere physical pain.

Still. This wasn't the worst part.

With the mantle destroyed, the Exir would be left exposed, unprotected. Our Nherum form deteriorated naturally when the Exir allowed it to die. Only when it was ready to be set free from its temporal vessel to a ceaseless existence. Until then, it couldn't survive without a vessel.

A luminous green light radiated from Alex's chest. Unnatural. Blinding, even for my eyes. But it was impossible to look away from the entrancing fusion of pain and beauty. *This* would be the worst part. Killing the immortal.

A sound pierced my ears, thick and sharp, overflowing with grief. The scream didn't come from Alex's physical voice; it was the wail of his wasting Exir. At the same time, Dru collapsed on the ground. He was nowhere near the tree that directly felt Alex's pain, but he must have felt its impact. Apart from the violent pulsation of the veins on his forehead, his entire body was rigid. His lips were pursed tightly, yet trembling as he struggled to hold back a screech clawing its way out of his throat.

Dru seemed to be in more pain now than when he was in direct contact with the tree. I knelt down and placed my hands on his shoulders to contain him. There was nothing logical about it, but somehow, I thought staying still would ease his pain.

My attempt was useless. Dru trembled more violently until he could no longer hold back. But still, he didn't scream. Instead, he exhaled with harsh sobs. The pain inside of him and around him had completely taken over. With both hands pressed hard on his ears, he seemed to be trying desperately to block the sound of pain from each wailing tree.

Leaves began to fall from the surrounding trees that trembled like Dru. Alex's pain was so strong that every single tree around us seemed to feel it without physical contact. I looked up at the one tree that touched Alex's decayed body; there were no leaves left in the shriveled dry branches.

The rays of green light that peeked through the gaps between Alex's festered fingers were accompanied by the warmest shade of orange. Sunset was leaking from his chest. The light grew stronger until it illuminated the surrounding woods, until we were inside his sunset. His Exir was burning. It was tragic. It was magnificent.

This was it. The burning. The explosion. I held my breath as the light moved into circular motion around Alex's hand. It moved faster as it worked its way up to bigger loops around his still body, diffusing into a full sized, blazing tornado of emerald and fire.

But the tornado didn't stir anything. Not a single falling leaf was interrupted from its rapid journey to the ground. There was no wind, just light, striking light. Its movement, despite the speed and the force of a tornado, seemed to sway elegantly to the sound that it produced: the most soothing melodic hum.

This was the sound of the Exir, fighting to live. But it was meant to lose, and this glorious site was meant to fade away. I wanted to remember every single detail, every loop, shade, tone, note.

I didn't blink as I gazed at the magnificence that grew weaker and weaker. Its movement slowed down, and the loops broke up into tiny flickers of shattered Exir. In just a few heartbeats, we were surrounded by hundreds of fiery emerald sparks floating in the air, in a gradual sacred descend. The musical hum began to fade with every spark that hit the ground.

My brain was lost in astonishment. I didn't know how long we stood motionless after the explosion, completely captivated by the beautiful tragedy.

I should feel more resentment. I shouldn't be able to understand why a creature that was completely aware of his sanctity would insist on embracing the most unnatural, agonizing end. But as I watched the last spark of his Exir smash on the ground to expire, I felt his peace.

I didn't mind staying here for longer than necessary. I stood still and breathed in the serenity Alex had left behind. For the first time since Scarlett had taken over my mind, I didn't feel like I was falling in a dark hole with so much force around me that I had no control of my senses. In this moment, at least, I felt stable.

Dru was also still, perhaps for a different reason. He would have needed time to recover from Alex's pain. He drew sharp breaths until he was ready to speak. "What did he mean?" Dru's voice sounded weak and broken.

"I don't know," I lied.

"The human," he said, ignoring my pathetic denial.

It wasn't a question, but I answered in a forged factual tone, "No."

"You're in danger."

"He could have been talking to you," I threw a feeble defense at him.

"Do you believe that?"

"No."

"Then tell me everything." The patience in Dru's eyes told me he knew I wasn't quite ready to start talking. I needed strength to get through this. I needed to jump. Without a second thought, I shot up into the air in search of the serenity I desperately needed back.

I couldn't find it. I was soaring, but a part of me was falling fast and deep, back into the dark hole. I kept jumping anyway. Each time my feet sprung off the ground, I felt free from my obligation to Dru. I knew it was inevitable, but I jumped as long as he allowed me to. I needed to stay high up in the air, and I didn't care about my direction, or how close I came to the city. I could sense Dru following me, perhaps making sure I didn't end up somewhere I shouldn't be. I laughed darkly to myself at the thought of how our roles had reversed. I was supposed to be the one overseeing him, but there he was, following me with tension in his heartbeat, preparing to contain my erratic behavior.

Dru caught up with me when I was a couple of feet off the ground for another jump. He placed his right hand on my shoulder to push me down. "That's enough, Pete." He stood behind me with his hand still resting heavily on my shoulder. From the force he exerted to keep me in place, I knew he was no longer willing to let me go. Dru had gradually gained his strength back as we moved away from the place of Alex's death, but he was still weak. I could overpower him, but I couldn't jump forever.

I wasn't afraid to face him. Fear wasn't the reason of my hesitation. It was shame. This must be why Alex hid himself in the shadows of the forest. He ran without looking back, unable to face his kind. However, unlike Alex, I hadn't committed the sin. I shouldn't bear the same shame.

"Okay." I nodded.

"You have to face this," Dru said when he lifted his hand from my shoulder.

"I know." I'd never be truly ready to do this, but I had to try. It had to be now. Dru moved back and sat on an elevated root of a tree behind us. I didn't move. I couldn't even turn to face him.

"I don't know what to tell you."

"The truth."

"Her eyes are the shade of leaves between summer and autumn."

"How does she make you feel?"

"Insane." If I was going to do this, I had to be completely honest.

"Do you feel a certain urge to be close to her?"

"Always. She's in my head. All the time." I almost wanted to smile at the beautiful image in my mind.

"Do you feel weak around her? Do you lose control?"

"Yes." This was the hardest to admit.

"Do you want to touch her?"

I hesitated for a few moments. "I don't know why."

"Do you think about the—"

"No," I interrupted. It was the truth. I had never felt the need to think about the *Forbidden* when I was with Scarlett.

"All the other indications are clear."

I was surprised at how well he managed to hide the panic in his voice.

"I'd never, I could never hurt her," I stated in a low voice that was almost a whisper.

"What did you say?" Astonishment replaced Dru's panic.

"You heard."

"You care about this human?"

"I do. More than I ever thought I could," I said in the same moment I realized the extent of how I felt.

"I don't understand."

"Neither do I," I said, with a humorless laugh that only highlighted the pain of my frustration.

"It's too risky. We don't know what we're dealing with here. You have to stay away."

I wanted to say it wasn't going to be possible for me to stay away from Scarlett. I was, quite simply, physically incapable of it. Of course, saying this wouldn't help me in showing Dru I could handle the situation. "Yes, you're right. For now, I don't know exactly what I'm going through. I have no answers, but isn't that why we're here in this world? To understand? We have a chance to be enlightened. Would you really want me to walk away from that?"

I held my breath as I waited for him to speak, but he was silent.

"Dru, you can't tell the others. Not yet. This is something I have to face alone. Please." I was done pretending. I let my composure drop as I turned to face him. He had the right to see how important this was to me.

He hesitated for a moment and said, "I can't let you do that."

I had to lift my hands to support my head. The thought of others knowing made if feel unbearably heavy. They'd say I was jeopardizing our mission, and I'd have to leave. I'd have to go back to my world and face my kind as a failure. *I would never see her again.*

The last thought hit me with such sharpness. I physically flinched as I felt its sting. "It's over," I said, defeated.

"Yes, it is. You won't have to deal with this on your own anymore"—he paused and said something that sounded like—"because I will help you figure this out."

I was sure I misheard him. The desperation must be causing my brain to fluctuate, but I didn't ask him to clarify. Every moment he didn't speak meant I could continue to be *hopeful*, something I learned from Scarlett.

"Now, you have to tell me everything that happened, every word, every physical reaction, every emotion. Everything."

There were no words enough to express how grateful I was, so I leaped onto a branch and began to tell the story of the human girl who made me weak.

I could no longer deny the danger I had to face whenever I was near Scarlett—the risk of losing Dru's trust, my place in this world, and my own life.

But I promised Scarlett I'd meet her the next day, so I stood outside her classroom and waited. I spent most of the night with Dru, analyzing my interactions with Scarlett and preparing myself for today, but when the door opened, she greeted me with a warm smile I wasn't used to. Then, I fell into a complete and utter vulnerability. She could have me. She could destroy me, shatter the immortal inside of me—I didn't care. I was hers. She could do whatever she wanted. I was all hers.

IV. DISCOVERY

The last three months had been a crucial time for learning. The more time I spent with Scarlett, the clearer it became it wasn't only her arresting gaze that contaminated my sanity. She had me in so many other ways. Hundreds of idiosyncrasies—from the way she crinkled her nose when she laughed to the way she bit her lower lip when she was deep in thought—interfered with the rhythm of my heartbeat.

Dru continued to help me analyze my connection with her. He even began to interact with humans, further assisting in our study of their effect on us.

Each moment with Scarlett was still unpredictable. Each word, each gesture affected me in so many ways that my existence had been perpetually encrusted with ambivalence. Her effect on me remained a mystery, but I no longer feared it. In fact, I found pleasure in the weakness her presence brought upon me. Dru, on the other hand, was concerned about this unpredictability because the lack of control meant greater risk of committing the *Forbidden*. This was a sentiment I'd chosen to ignore. I couldn't let Dru's unstable confidence in me impede my chance to be near Scarlett, especially since she no longer seemed to mind.

Waiting for Scarlett outside the tube station every morning had become habitual. She also spent some of her free periods with me. It meant I missed some of my own classes, but I decided Scarlett had more to teach me than any human academic.

At lunchtimes, we walked together to the crowded cafeteria. Unlike the tube station, I could follow her here.

Watching her go to the underground transport didn't get any easier with time. No matter how hard I tried to convince myself I could do it, I could finally go with her, my entire Nherum form persisted in its defiance.

I tried to make up for this physical limitation as much as I could. I did everything she allowed me to do for her; carried her books, sat beside her in British Romanticism, got the orange juice she liked to drink every morning . . . I wanted to do so much more to ensure she didn't have to waste her limited energy, but there were so many things she wouldn't let me do for her.

When I found out it was common human practice to give gifts as a way of showing appreciation, I seized the opportunity. This required taking a trip to the shops. The mere thought of stepping into another confined space with more humans than I cared to be in proximity with was enough to spark some apprehension. Nevertheless, I was motivated to obtain a palpable object that could show Scarlett even a fraction of my appreciation. When it came to this matter, I could never seem to articulate myself.

I began with what usually came natural to me—logic. Winter was fast approaching, so clothing articles to keep her warm seemed a good idea. However, choosing the most appropriate ones proved somewhat challenging. I had to ensure I selected the most durable and efficient materials without settling for either fabrics of inferior quality or animal fur. *This was another significant human flaw*, I thought to myself as I examined a pair of shoes made of lambskin, *They insisted on the unnecessary.* There was no good reason why they'd need to slaughter animals when they had the technology to create materials that could keep them just as warm and comfortable.

I had eight shopping bags in my hand when I stood in the middle of the street, thinking I had gone about this all wrong. Why did I think Scarlett would need more winter clothes than she already had? There was nothing in the shopping bags good enough to show the depth of my appreciation.

What could I give her that would tell her just how important she was to me?

Nothing.

It was almost time for the shops to close when it struck me. I'd never find something that would show her true worth to me, but I could give her something to remind her I was always thinking about her.

I was relieved to find the least crowded shop on the street. Apart from the sales assistants, the only other person in the shop was a man in a black suit, closely examining a ring. It didn't take me long to find the item. It was radiant, yet so simple, so discrete.

"Are you looking for anything in particular, sir?"

I looked up to find a shop assistant standing on the other side of the glass display, leaning a little too close to me, smiling a little too wide.

"Yes, I'd like to have a look at this one, please." I had to repeat myself before she finally leaned back and took her eyes off me.

"The base is platinum, encrusted with diamonds, two carats all together. Lucky girl," the shop assistant said.

Lucky. I shook my head. Luck was nothing more than another excuse for humans to expect finding themselves in a favorable situation, without effort. I kept my eyes on the item, avoiding the prying eyes of the shop assistant who continued to invade my private space by leaning too close. Even after I handed her back the item so I could pay for it, her gaze remained fixed on me for a few more seconds. Her face filled with an expression a part of me hoped to see on Scarlett's when I gave her my token of appreciation.

During lunch period the next day, I asked Scarlett to walk with me to my car. "Is this your car?" she asked, clearly surprised—though not impressed—to find the clear-coated carbon and polished aluminum car amongst the line of tiny hatchbacks.

"Yes, it is."

"Where do you even get a car like this? And how are you allowed to park in the staff's parking lot?" I was about to attempt to answer her questions as truthfully as I could, but to my relief, she added, "You know what, don't answer that. I don't think I want to know."

"These are for you." I picked up a couple of bags and gestured to the rest in the car.

"What the hell?" She frowned, glancing at the jumpers in the bags I held out to her. Instead of taking them, she asked, "Why?"

This wasn't a good start.

"I just wanted to give you something to show how much I appreciated your company," I said, explaining what I thought was an obvious, typical human custom.

"Are you out of your mind?" she exclaimed with a humorless laugh.

The uncertainty in her tone made me nervous. "I thought you might need these because of the season, but of course you already have winter clothes. It was the first time I have ever done this. I just—"

"What? No, no." She shook her head. "I appreciate the thought, and you taking the time, but buying me things to show your appreciation of my *company?* Do you know how that sounds?"

I did not.

"I just thought these would keep you warm," I said in an apologetic voice as I tried to accept the rejection I still didn't understand. How could something as simple as giving a gift be so complicated in this world?

"I don't need all these expensive designer labels to keep

me warm." There was no more offense in her tone, which gave me just enough confidence to pursue my intention.

"There's something else." I took the box from my coat pocket and opened it before I lost my nerve.

"Petyr . . ." she said hesitantly, shaking her head once again.

"Please, take no notice of who made it. That's irrelevant. I want you to know that no matter what the time is, you can call me, and I'll be there for you."

Her expression was better than the shop assistant's. Scarlett's had depth and sincerity. She allowed me to take her hand and replace the watch with worn leather strap.

As we walked to the cafeteria, Scarlett looked at me and said, "Next time you feel like telling me something, just say it. No props necessary." She took my hand, locked her fingers with mine and added, "Saves you filling up your car with shopping bags." Her lighthearted smile didn't prevent me from feeling too weak to even breathe as I felt the warmth of her palm against mine. She found another way to ensure I was incapable of anything but submission. She could have asked me anything, and I'd have answered truthfully.

This was also the day when I started to eat human food. I'd been getting away with just having a bottle of fizzy drink or a cup of coffee while Scarlett had her lunch. When she asked me why I didn't get any food for myself, I'd say I wasn't hungry. It was almost the truth, but I couldn't be completely honest and say I was *never* hungry.

This day, however, she didn't ask me the question. Instead, she ordered me, "You should eat something." The combination of firmness and concern in her voice had made it very difficult for me to refuse.

"I should," I said, watching her face glow with another combination of expressions. As if one wasn't enough to confound me.

The cafeteria food was far from tolerable. I felt a twist in my stomach as I approached the counter where the greasy, mutilated meat was placed on display. I thought of what Dru would do if he could see through my eyes. I wondered if Nero, who made a point of having at least one meal a day, could stand to eat deep-fried chicken. I certainly couldn't. I stuck to the fruits and vegetables, and after a week, Scarlett asked me if I was a vegetarian.

"I guess I am."

She laughed softly and asked, "You guess?"

"It wasn't really an option for me. I didn't decide to be one. It's just what felt right," I explained as honestly as I could.

"You're extraordinary," she said in the low, warm tone that never failed to send some sort of electric current in my veins.

Extraordinary. She often used the word to describe me, and each time, she said it like she could see through me. We'd spent almost every day of the last three months together, and she still didn't know who I was. I should be proud of myself for keeping up my pretense this long, but now that she looked at me, and her smiles were no longer forced, and her voice often formed the sound of my name . . . I wanted more. I wanted her to know me, everything about me. I'd thought of telling her, but my fear of losing her didn't allow me the strength to step out of the safety of my lies.

I waited outside the tube station on a damp Monday morning, with a bottle of orange juice in one hand and an umbrella in the other. After having spent two whole days without Scarlett, I was especially impatient on Monday mornings. With great difficulty, I fought the urge to jump into the tunnel, pull the train faster to the station, force the doors open, and lift her out of the crowded carriage. Knowing I could be standing on this same spot with Scarlett in just a matter of seconds made the next eighteen minutes and thirty-seven seconds even more arduous. When our eyes met, her face radiated with a smile that told me she was glad to see me too. The last eighteen minutes and thirty-seven seconds—and the last two days, for that matter—became instantly irrelevant.

"Thanks, but again, you didn't have to," Scarlett said when I gave her the orange juice.

"You know it's my pleasure," I replied, holding the umbrella over her. She looked exquisite in a lavender coat that was considerably thicker than the one she normally wore.

"Aren't you cold in that?" she asked, throwing a glance at my gray jumper.

"Freezing," I replied with my eyes fixed on my shoes to avoid her gaze. This was one of those moments when I wished she knew the truth about me, so I didn't have to lie.

"So why aren't you wearing a coat?"

"I didn't think it was necessary," I said, trying to be honest.

"You better put this on before you catch a cold or something." She removed the scarf from her neck and handed it to me. "It should keep you a little warmer, though it might ruin the magazine cover look you got going on," she added with a playful smile.

Scarlett had never reacted to my physical appearance the way most female humans did, so I wasn't quite sure how to respond to her comment. She gave me another playful smile and handed me the bottle of orange juice, "You should have some of this too, Vitamin C."

I wanted her to have the rest of the juice, but I took the bottle, tempted by the opportunity to share something with her. I held it tight in my hand. This was something that belonged to both of us. Somehow I felt a different kind of connection with her. We were no longer on opposite sides. For now, at least, we were standing on the same exact spot. It was an extremely intricate feeling even my mind couldn't rationalize completely, but it made me realize how far I'd come since the day my mind was taken over by the image of the girl who never looked at me.

Autumn seemed to have come and gone overnight. There were hardly any dried leaves left to cover the green memories of the summer. The grass was frosted with the reflection of the gray sky. Scarlett seemed to be the only vibrant figure in this dull, misty picture.

"You make everything better." A simple 'thank you' would have been a more appropriate thing to say, but I wanted her to know what I really thought. After all, opportunities to be honest with her didn't come by often.

She laughed. "Well, I can't make you better if you fall ill, so don't forget your coat tomorrow."

"I won't," I promised.

She smiled tentatively at what would have sounded like an empty promise. For her to appreciate the real extent of my honesty, she would first have to be aware I could neither fall ill nor forget.

What was the point of my continuous attempt at honesty if everything was ultimately overshadowed by the lie that was my entire identity?

Before I, once again, entertained the temptation of revealing everything, I tried to distract myself by focusing on another chance to spend more time with her. "When do you want to meet up to prepare for our presentation on poetry?"

"How about tomorrow? If you want, we can go to the library after my class."

"Sounds good." It sounded much more than good, but I had three months of practice, and I was beginning to show real progress.

The next day, I leaned on the wall opposite Scarlett's classroom door and waited for it to open. I didn't like waiting very much. Still, I arrived half an hour early. My impatience to see her again always caused me to leave the house too early. Dru would suggest that a part of me liked the torture of knowing she was only a few feet away from me, hidden by the wall I could easily remove from my sight if I wasn't trying so hard to do the right thing these days. The temptation to omit the wall from my sight was always there. *Just a glance*, a voice in my mind would say, *One short glance couldn't hurt*. I had to resist the persuasion of my own irrational mind. Ultimately, the door always opened. She always stepped out with the bright smile that made the torture of waiting worthwhile.

This time, however, the torture dragged on. No bright smile. No Scarlett.

"Where was she?" I whispered to myself. This was the wrong question to ask. My mind had hundreds of possible answers for it: she could've fallen ill because I'd taken her scarf yesterday; she could've been in an accident; she could've been attacked on the way home last night, and I wasn't there to protect her because I was too much of a coward to ride the tube; she could have . . .

Stop.

I rushed to my car as fast as my human façade would allow me. I always made a point of leaving my mobile phone in the car, just in case the others decided to call while I was with Scarlett. Apart from Dru, they still didn't know about her, and she didn't know about them. Telling Scarlett about the others would mean having to lie about my relationship with them. I had already told her too many lies. I wasn't willing to add more if I could help it.

There were two missed calls and a text message on my mobile phone. She made the first phone call twenty-four minutes ago. If only I'd tried harder to control my impulse, I wouldn't have gotten to her classroom too early. I could have answered her call. I sighed as I read her message.

Hey, I'll have to cancel. My little brother is not well, so I have to stay home with him. I hope you read this message before you set off. Sorry. —Scarlett

Despite what the message said, I had to hear her voice to believe she was all right. I dialed. It rang. No answer. I dialed again. It rang. No answer. I dialed again. It rang.

"Hello?"

I allowed myself to feel the relief I didn't deserve. "Hi, it's Petyr."

"Hey, did you get my message?"

"Yes, are you all right? How's your brother?"

"He has a little fever, but he's fine. I'm sorry to have to bail on you like that. My parents had already left for work when Jack's school called."

"No, please, don't worry about it." The apparent guilt in her voice made me cringe. I made a promise to always be there for her, and I couldn't even answer her call. "I can come to you."

She paused.

I held my breath.

She sighed.

My lungs drowned in unwanted air.

"You don't have to do that."

"I'll come over if you want me to."

"Number 18, Pinley Road . . ." I could picture her smile as she told me her address.

"I'll be there as soon as I can." I started the car before she'd even put the phone down. I got to her street in less than fifteen minutes, but I waited for ten more before I made my way to her door.

Scarlett greeted me with a wide smile and said, "How many stoplights did you run to get here this fast?"

"Not as many as you'd think."

Once again, her presence had drowned all of my guilt. She had an astounding way of making me forget about my foolishness. She was my absolute serenity. She made everything good. Incredibly overwhelming and confusing and daunting, but good.

As Scarlett welcomed me into the place she called home, I wished I could do the same for her. I wished I could let her into my world, but I was grateful to be here. A large painting of a bird sitting on a tree branch caught my attention, not just because it was far too big for such a narrow hallway. Its deep, black eyes exuded a sense of misery. It didn't belong. It wasn't flying.

"I'm sorry about that. My parents have hideous taste in art," she said with a playful smile, though it failed to hide her embarrassment.

"It's interesting."

"It's a bird."

"You don't like birds?"

"I don't like that painting. It's not really my taste."

"So what is your taste?"

"Better," she replied lightheartedly.

"I'm sure," I said in a more serious tone than I'd intended.

She flashed a smile, reminding me that despite the serenity I felt when she was around, she hadn't lost the power to take my breath away.

I followed her through a door to the living room, cramped with two oversized green fabric sofas and matching chairs, a round wooden coffee table, two side tables, bookshelves, paintings, and numerous ornaments. There were urns of different sizes on the tables and even on the floor, wooden sculptures, crystals, and figurines. The unrelated ornaments seemed to have been acquired as a collection of souvenirs rather than decorations.

"You travel a lot." I decided that showing certainty in my conclusion, instead of saying the same phrase in a form of a question, was a step closer to being myself.

"I know it looks like a gift-shop in here. My parents love to drag us to different countries for a four-week holiday every summer. There's nothing worse than being stuck to go gift-shop hopping with the parents. At least now I'm eighteen, I get to say no."

"Do you?" I asked, wondering if this practice applied to all human families.

She laughed. "Fine, fine, I haven't actually attempted to say no yet, but a girl can dream."

The flexible rules in this world didn't help in my attempt to understand the humans. "Don't you like to discover new places?"

"Not really. They're just places—buildings, roads, trees. They might look a little different, but they're all the same."

"I'm sure one day you'll find a place unique enough to impress you," I replied, deluding myself that there was even a remote possibility Scarlett could see my world. Before I could allow myself to further hope for the impossible, I turned my attention to a child sitting on the sofa with a blanket over him.

"Jack! What did we agree on just now?" Scarlett asked with authority and affection, a combination I hadn't heard from her before.

"I know, I know, no more cartoons, but you left, and I got bored," he replied without taking his eyes off the television.

"I'd only been gone a couple of seconds!" she exclaimed. This time, the authority in her voice was replaced by amusement.

"It was longer." He shrugged.

"Fine, but that's it. Then you'll have to go to your room and get some rest. We don't want you falling asleep on the sofa again. It's not good for your back."

"I'm not tired!" he protested with a rather convincing attempt to sound energetic.

"The drowsy meds will kick in any minute," she said to me, and then she picked up the remote control from the coffee table and turned the television off. "Jack, let's go."

Ignoring Scarlett, Jack asked me, "Who are you?"

"I'm Petyr," I replied.

"Okay, but who are you?"

"I believe I just answered the question." I was unsure of what he expected me to say. It was the one question I couldn't answer truthfully.

"No you haven't." He must have learned a trick or two about being difficult to read from his sister.

"He's my friend," Scarlett interjected and continued with a wide grin, "He's here to help me look after you, aren't you, Petyr?"

"Yes, I suppose I could," I answered though I didn't understand the reason behind the grin.

"I don't like him," Jack announced and turned his back on me.

"Don't be rude," Scarlett warned him.

"You always tell me I shouldn't lie," he said casually.

"Jack! You know being polite isn't lying."

I could tell she meant to show more firmness, but her voice sounded more like a suggestion than reprimand. She attempted to give him a final meaningful look before turning to me. "I'm sorry. He's not in a very good mood because of the fever. He's not always this obnoxious. He's only six, but he usually has better manners."

"Don't worry about it. He's not wrong. He shouldn't lie." I could only wish I had the same privilege.

Scarlett gave me a faint smile then lightly shook her head the way she always did before she called me extraordinary. She didn't say the word this time. Instead, she reached for my hand. Naturally, this was a direct order for my heart to start expanding inside my chest, for all of my weaknesses to manifest. But I refused to freeze until I took her hand and held it in mine. I could feel the blood rushing through her veins. No more denying it. Yes, I found pleasure in feeling weak.

Every increased heartbeat, every confused thought, every drop of anxiety, every ounce of fear, every single moment I spent helpless in the captivation of her eyes brought an addictive, exhilarating pleasure. Alas, it took only a single rustling sound for Scarlett to let go.

"Jack, seriously?" She made an open gesture with her

hands, throwing her palms upward. I'd noticed this was the same gesture humans used when they asked for something, when they drew attention to their surroundings, or when they were unable to furnish an answer to a question.

"I'm hungry," Jack replied with great efforts to sound feeble as he clutched onto a bag of crisps.

"Nice try. You just had your lunch. C'mon, pal, let's get you some rest." Scarlett said, using the same gesture to ask Jack for the bag of crisps.

I got to my feet, but Jack turned to me and said, "Only people I like are allowed in my room."

"Jack!" Scarlett exclaimed, giving her brother a look I interpreted as a warning of some sort, and then she turned to me apologetically. "He doesn't mean it."

"He's not being unreasonable. I'll just wait down here. It's no problem at all," I assured her. I waited for thirteen minutes and twenty-nine seconds before I heard Scarlett's light footsteps down the stairs.

"Hey, sorry to keep you waiting again. He can be really stubborn sometimes and—"

"Don't worry about it," I interrupted before she apologized again for something that wasn't her fault. "You have a lot of interesting things in here to keep me occupied."

"Interesting." She chuckled. "You're too polite. Don't worry, they're not my things, you can say tacky."

"I don't know about tacky, but I guess you're right. Nothing in here is particularly interesting to me. That is to say, nothing here says much about you."

"You've been trying to spy on me?" She tried to sound offended, but the smile refused to leave her face.

I returned her smile and nodded. "And failing."

"That's because you're looking in the wrong place. C'mon," she said with a gesture, which I took to be an indication that she wanted me to follow her. I was becoming increasingly familiar with the non-verbal signals humans used. We headed up the stairs, through a hallway, and up another set of stairs.

"Here you go. Let the espionage commence," she teased when we entered her room.

It was a compact, isolated area on the top floor. Yet, the ivory walls, cream curtains and windows on the slanted roof made it seem considerably bright and spacious. As I stepped into the room, I found myself standing beside a wooden desk that was particularly organized. The laptop was only a couple of centimeters off the center of the table. The box of paper clips, staples, and stapler were carefully aligned on the right-hand corner. The strong scent of lemon made it evident the surface was freshly polished. In fact, the scent of artificial lemon exuded from the rest of the wooden furniture in the room. I felt peculiarly comfortable inside Scarlett's uncluttered world.

"Are you planning on standing there all day?"

I was taken aback by her question. I didn't have a plan, but yes, I could stand here all day. In fact, I could stay here for a lot longer than a day.

"I wouldn't mind."

"You're crazy." She laughed her melodious laugh that never failed to draw a smile out of me.

"You aren't the first one to notice," I replied. Dru's comments with regards to my sanity echoed in my head.

"Then I guess I should be worried, but what the hell." She moved to the middle of the bed and tapped the space she'd just freed up. No logic connected the gesture to its supposed meaning. Yet, it seemed natural for me to move closer and sit next to her on the bed.

"I-I guess we better get started with the research." Something unexpected happened when she uttered the words. She panicked. Her eyes avoided mine. She flipped the pages with more force than necessary. "It's here somewhere."

I could sense her frustration as she searched for Samuel Taylor Coleridge's section in the book of Romantic poets. I knew the page she was looking for, so I decided to help her locate it. My calculated movements ensured my hand would reach the book without interrupting the motion of hers.

I should have known that, with Scarlett, nothing was ever calculated. As soon as I moved, she stopped flipping the pages. Scarlett's eyes found my hand frozen in mid-air. Slowly, I reached for the book and located the page with Coleridge's poetry.

I intended to pull my intrusive hand back as fast as I could, hoping she would forgive my interruption. Once again, she caught me by surprise. Before I could even move an inch, I felt her cold hand over mine. She was nervous. It was remarkable how the humans' lack of control over their physical bodies made some things very predictable. As the words *human* and *predictable* echoed in my mind, I allowed myself to smile at the irony, a smile Scarlett claimed and returned. The smile wasn't initially for her, but it was hers to claim. All of my smiles were hers, and everything else she wanted from me.

I didn't panic. Even with her commanding eyes and paralyzing touch, I was able to move this time. I felt liberty to pursue the intense yearning to grab her hand and pull her toward me.

My actions were motivated by the desire I didn't know I had. It wasn't something I understood, but I recognized it. I had seen the same desire too many times on faces that gaped upon my physical appearance. It was the same, yet stronger, much, *much* stronger. Strong enough to push me towards her until my face was less than an inch away from hers. Strong enough to break the cautious chain that kept me from running my fingers across her warm cheeks, down her delicate neck, through her soft curls, along her curved back. Strong enough to intoxicate me as I leaned closer and pressed my lips against hers.

I fought to hear the rational thoughts in my mind, but it wasn't a fight I wanted to win. I was drowning in the violent sea that permitted no rationalizations, no calculation, only desire. Every part of my brain was focused on this moment, on Scarlett. A part felt her increasing temperature. A part monitored every slow, heavy breath. A part kept me from shaking with every blazing touch. A part held on to the last thread of sanity as her lips were enmeshed with mine. A part listened to her heartbeat . . .

I placed my hand on her chest to feel the erratic beats. I needed to assure myself she was real, and it was possible to feel such elation, such sublimity.

Elation.

Sublimity.

No.

I wished I could ignore the implication of these words, but the faint distant voice in my head was becoming clearer with each heartbeat.

I wasn't ready to be revived. Until I let myself acknowledge the connection, I wouldn't have to accept it. I desperately needed to keep drowning.

But I was saved. Against my will, I was saved by a thunder in my head. A weak, husky voice struck me back to my senses.

Sublimity at its highest, elation no creature in any world can even dream of. How can I regret that?

Alex's words convicted me of the very sin I'd been entrusted to eradicate. But he was wrong. I felt remorse. It crept through my veins and dissolved every last bit of errant desire. I regretted my ignorance for not knowing I could be intoxicated. I could drown. I could lose control.

I was capable of committing the *Forbidden*.

I'd give anything for just one more second of sublimity—

anything but Scarlett. In this moment, two things could happen. I could use what little strength I had to walk away from her, or I could succumb to the *Forbidden* and take both her life and mine. One thing was for certain. I would lose her.

The thought of spending centuries without seeing her face or hearing her voice instigated pain so potent, so palpable. For one brief second, I needed to be selfish. I needed to choose to die with her than live without her.

But something held me back. A force, compelling me to protect her. It was far stronger than my selfish need to protect myself from the pain of losing her. The pain cut through my chest as I pulled away from Scarlett. I couldn't take anything away from her, certainly not her life.

She gazed at me with affection I didn't deserve. I had to look away. I was no longer worthy of her warm captivation. All I could manage was a feeble whisper. "I'm sorry." Then I rushed out of her room, her house, her life.

Without checking if anyone was around to see, I jumped. I barely touched the ground when I sprung back into the air. I had no intention to stop jumping. If I spent even a full second on land, I wouldn't be strong enough to stop myself from going back to Scarlett. I kept jumping until I landed in front of a car parked in the middle of a road. I didn't need to see through the tinted windows to know who was inside.

"I should have known you'd be chasing me," I whispered, knowing she would hear me even though I stood almost five yards away from the car.

She didn't reply immediately. Instead, she rolled down the dark window. The smile on her face didn't make sense. A smile on Kara's face wasn't something that appeared regularly, and it was certainly not something I'd expect to see considering the present circumstances.

You need to talk to me. She didn't speak, but I heard every word. Kara's nature allowed her the ability to push words into someone else's mind. Making sure they were always heard was one of the many ways Kara's Corta showed superiority over others.

I resented the way her voice invaded my mind. I could easily stop her from imposing her false sense of superiority over me, but I had more important things to deal with than pride.

"I need a lot of things right now, but talking to you is not one of them." My bitter response didn't wipe the smile from her face.

"You need me," she said in the most pleasant manner I had ever heard from her, or any of her kind for that matter.

"I have everything under control," I lied.

"Are you sure about that?" she asked, though her tone suggested she knew everything that happened. Instead of exploding in rage and condemning me for the disgrace I was, she addressed me with a lighthearted tease. Nothing made sense to me anymore. I no longer cared enough to try. What was the point of attempting to hide my failure? I walked to the car to face my fate.

Kara picked up her phone. "He's worse than you think." She laughed coldly. "He didn't even try to outwit me. It was pathetic. You'll see for yourself in a few minutes." She hung up when I got into the car and started the engine.

"Who was that?"

"So the human really broke you, huh? You can't even function to figure out something so simple?"

I didn't respond. Yes, I was broken, more than she could ever understand.

"Nero." Kara finally answered my question to end the silence.

"He finally solved his mystery." I sighed. Nero had won.

"You're the only one in the dark," she said with a meaningful smile that I didn't understand.

"I don't care."

"You still have it in you to figure it out, broken as you are." Maybe she was right, but I didn't care. It was too late.

I'd lost Scarlett.

When we got to the shared house, Dru was the first to speak. "We got it wrong."

"I guess you've been enlightened," I replied without attempting to hide the cold disappointment in my voice.

"Yes, I have, and so will you," he said through a wide beam.

"Enough!" I was certain I had almost committed the *Forbidden*, yet I stood in front of three optimistic faces. I was troubled by what their present dispositions stirred within me: hope. "What do I have to do?"

Though I was asking myself more than anyone else, Nero responded, "You have to understand what you feel." His voice wasn't embedded with conceit.

"I feel exactly like someone who'd almost killed a human should, someone who'd almost jeopardized the security of our kind, someone—"

"You didn't," Dru interrupted my confession.

"Dru," Nero said with controlled calmness, allowing just enough rigidity in his tone to send a momentary surge of silence in the room.

"Give him a break!" Dru protested, but Nero's expression was an evident warning that it wasn't Dru's place to say any more.

"Fine." Dru sighed reluctantly and turned to me, "But let me just say this. It's impossible to pull away from the *Forbidden*."

"I did."

Both Dru and Nero gave me a moment to decipher the situation, and normally a moment was more than enough. Kara seemed to know I needed more this time. She was in the kitchen, peeling an orange she didn't intend to eat when she pushed a question into my head. *Did you?*

"She's alive, and I'm unharmed." Her futile question aggravated my impatience.

Yes, you are. Her voice echoed in my mind, and a drop of pure clarity washed through my hazy thoughts.

To walk away from the *Forbidden* was to overcome the impossible. With all my strength, this wasn't something I was capable of, let alone in a weakened, intoxicated state.

It was all about Scarlett—the desire that consumed me was merely the need to feel her, to hear her, to be close to her . . .

I was not in danger of the *Forbidden*, but I was in danger of something equally aberrant.

I was in love.

V. REVELATION

I knew what love was. It was an illusion, a mere excuse for the humans' illogical need to reproduce their feeble race.

It wasn't supposed to be a genuine force powerful enough to overcome me, especially not powerful enough to shield me from the *Forbidden*. I couldn't deny that I did feel the temptation of the *Forbidden*. I felt its pull, but I was able to fight it because of how I felt for Scarlett, because of love.

As the first of my kind to experience human love, I should focus the best part of my brain on evaluating the potential threats this new discovery could bring to our race.

The humans had thousands of ways to describe love, but the words from one of Coleridge's poems Scarlett and I were supposed to study for our presentation accentuated the surge of emotions I felt for her.

You mould my Hopes, you fashion me within;
And to the leading Love-throb in the Heart
Thro'all my Being, thro my pulse's beat;
You lie in all my many Thoughts, like Light,
Like the fair light of Dawn, or summer Eve
On rippling Stream, or cloud-reflecting Lake.

As the lines resonated in my mind, it was almost hard to believe I didn't, until now, acknowledge how much I did love her. She changed me. She taught me to hope. Every part of my being screamed for her. She crept into my thoughts until everything, even the most desolate corner of my mind, was wrapped in her light.

Nero's self-righteous fashion was only too soon to return. He pointed out how he recognized the possibility that I could be falling in love with a human before anyone else could. His remarks were likely aimed to establish his triumph over Kara, who was supposed to perceive the unexpected. To my ears though, his words were nothing but a reminder of my failure to recognize the truth about my own situation.

"Not everyone is foolish enough to rush into announcing an abstract suspicion." Kara retorted to Nero's condescending remarks. I could tell her defensive words were in aid of me. Perhaps Nero did deserve to be acknowledged for his perception, but seeing his face as Kara casually referred to him as a fool was far too satisfying.

Nero knew how to pick his battles though. It didn't take someone of our Corta to recognize it wasn't ever a good idea to engage in a spiteful exchange against Kara, or anyone from her Corta for that matter. Perhaps in an attempt to maintain his authority, he moved on to what he would expect to be an easier target: Dru. "A simple cooperation would have gone a long way in making this easier for everyone."

"You think going behind Petyr's back would have made things easier? You could have told us what you thought. Instead, you let us waste time for three months just so you could gloat," Dru protested, but he was unable to conceal the guilt in his voice.

"It's so much easier to see the big picture when you're outside of it." I broke my silence to remind Dru the guilt wasn't his to bear.

I could feel the tolerance I was welcomed with rapidly fading. It was clear the only thing keeping the others from declaring our most rational move—which was to go back to our world and seek the help of Evan—was their interest in hearing what I planned to do.

I did have a plan. A simple one. I'd go back to Scarlett's house, and I'd tell her everything. I needed to find out if she felt the same way I did for her, and to do so, she needed to know me. Everything about me. What I was, where I came from, and the most difficult fact: *the reason I was here*.

I thought of every word I'd say, every tone, every gesture, every minute detail, but as soon as I imagined her standing in front of me, I stumbled. I was paralyzed by uncertainty—by fear that she wouldn't accept me. I couldn't move. I needed to stay in this moment where I had the liberty to hope. I sat still on the sofa longer than Nero and Kara were willing to wait. They'd left for their own apartments to do anything but waste time sitting still.

Dru stayed. He sat on the other end of the sofa, fidgeting restlessly and trying his best to appear like he wasn't there for me. Finally, he said in a quiet voice, "She hasn't got your time."

He was right. Every second I let my cowardice stop me from moving was a second wasted from Scarlett's fleeting existence. A subtle nod was all I could manage to give Dru.

With every jump, I became increasingly confident that I could do what I had to do, but as soon as I landed across the street from her house, my courage faltered.

Even though the lights in Scarlett's room were off, I knew she was awake as I listened to her breathing pattern.

I thought of Dru's words and, in spite of my trembling hands, I compelled myself to pick up a stone from the pavement. Throwing a stone up to her bedroom window was a far more discreet way of getting her attention than what I initially had in mind. It required me to jump and bang on the glass pane.

Scarlett drew the curtains open and stood behind the glass window. The certainty in her eyes was astounding. She knew I was there. Her expectant eyes searched the surroundings until they reached the spot where I was cowardly concealed in the darkness. She couldn't have seen anything more than a vague shape in the shadows, yet for a brief second, her sharp gaze pierced me.

"You've got to be kidding me." She sighed and stepped back. Had I been strong enough, I would have stepped out of my dim refuge and confessed before she could draw the curtains closed.

I needed something to pull me out of the paralyzing comfort of the shadows, to take away the fear. I listened, desperate to hear her utter at least one syllable that would help me know her mind. I heard every careless footstep thump rapidly against the wooden floor. I heard the tap whistle as water gushed through the pipes and crashed against the sink. I heard hinges screech as wardrobe doors flung open. I heard short heavy breaths supplemented by rapid erratic heartbeat, but not a single word. Not until the footsteps descended on the stairs and she finally appeared standing on the front porch, eyes fixed on me.

"What are you doing here?"

The tone of undeniable distress in her voice compelled me to step out of my shelter and walk toward her—faster than I should in front of a human. Speed was necessary for two reasons. I couldn't bear to let her feel the distress I caused any longer than I'd already done, and I relied on the momentum to give me the strength to move at all.

"Come with me," I said when I reached her front porch. I realized how ridiculous my request sounded to a human at 2:27 in the morning.

"Why should I? Why should I trust you?"

"You have no reason to. All I'm asking for is a chance to show you what I am. That doesn't make sense, I know, but—"

"No. I get it," she interrupted. "There's always been something about you that just doesn't add up. Show me what you've been trying so hard to hide."

I stepped closer to Scarlett and pulled her to me, securing her in my arms. It was easy. My arms automatically found the right place to ensure Scarlett would be safely supported.

It felt natural to hold her. "You might want to close your eyes," I whispered in her ear before I lifted us into the air.

I felt her urgent need for a gasp of air as she held her breath in our ascent. "I got you." My attempt to reassure her was ineffective. Her hands trembled as she endeavored to tighten her grip. For a few seconds, I relished the opportunity to pull her even closer so her body was pressed against mine. I could taste the scent of wild flowers and berries from the soft strands of her hair that brushed against my lips. I could feel fragments of her life with every warm breath on my chest. Her arms grasped me, like she never wanted to let go.

I never wanted to let go.

For a few brief seconds, it didn't matter that she didn't know everything about me. She belonged to me, and I was hers. I wished I could stay in this moment, ignore the signs, and pretend I wasn't aware of her fear.

I was heading to the forest where I could have the privacy and the space to show her all that I was. Fear weighed me down—both hers and mine. I knew she was afraid of what she didn't understand, but I was also afraid she would refuse to listen, deprive me of the chance to be honest. I had to stop. I had to place her back down on Earth where she belonged.

"I'm sorry," I whispered as we touched the ground in the middle of an unfamiliar residential area.

"Stop. You can't do this." Her voice was weak. She took a small step back, but I kept a firm hold of her hands.

It felt like something was about to pull her way from me. She wasn't ready for this. "I'll take you home, I'm sor—"

"No, stop," she interrupted.

"Please, don't worry, I won't . . . I'll drive."

She tried to pull her hands back, but mine refused to let hers go—desperate to hold on to her, to convince her not to be afraid.

"Drive what?"

I couldn't answer her question directly. I was too ashamed to admit I'd readily commit something her human values would consider an offense. All I could manage was a quick glance at one of the cars parked on the side of the road, but it was enough.

"You're going to steal—"

"Borrow," I corrected. "It will be returned."

"Sure, 'cause that's what you do, right? You disrupt something, you take it away, but it's okay because you can just effortlessly drop it right back!" The intensity in her tone made it apparent she was no longer talking about a car.

"I just don't want to scare you away."

"I'm not afraid," she whispered.

"I wish that were true." I sighed and ran my fingers down the side of her delicate face, fascinated by its complexity to bear so many emotions I couldn't fathom. But her ambivalence wasn't enough to cover the fear in her eyes.

"Why did you come back? I was so close to convincing myself to stop thinking about you, the disgusted expression on your face when you pulled away from me. And now you're doing it again. You whisk me off to something incredible just so you could drop me back down and walk away." Her words sparked the far too familiar sense of guilt and shame to resurface. I wanted to believe I was trying to protect her, but I walked away from her because *I* was afraid of what *I* didn't understand. I was afraid of how it would change *me*, ruin *me*. And now, I wanted to take her back home because I was afraid she wouldn't accept me.

I reached out to hold her, wishing my arms could absorb the pain I'd caused. It was mine. I should feel it, not her.

"I'm sorry." I could barely get the words out. I didn't deserve her forgiveness, but she had to know I didn't mean to hurt her.

"What do you want from me?" No more resentment in her voice, just genuine need for answers.

"I want you."

She closed her eyes for a moment, unsure of how to respond. "I need to know you. Who you are, what you are. I want to understand you," she said softly.

"I want you to know me, but I don't want to scare you away."

"I'm not scared of you. You can't keep walking away because you think I'm afraid, because you're afraid."

"I know." She was right. I was more afraid than she was.

"Don't confuse fear with my involuntary physical reactions to something I've never experienced before." The certainty in her voice commanded me to believe her.

I had to stop underestimating her because of my own fears. I slowly moved closer and lifted her into my arms. I kept one arm under her upper back and the other tucked behind her knees, hoping she would feel more secure this time. Once again, I jumped with her. When my feet were off the ground, she leaned her head on my chest, but she didn't close her eyes. Instead, she looked at me with a sparkle in her eyes that sent a familiar sensation. It weakened and strengthened me, all at once.

She could see me for what I was and, at least for now, she accepted me.

"Tell me everything," she said as soon as we landed in the middle of a forest outside London.

"I will tell you everything you want to know, but I think you should see what I am first. Then you can decide if you still want to know," I said, stepping a few paces back. I gave her a gentle smile before closing my eyes, hoping to convince her not to be afraid of what she was about to witness.

I began to focus my senses to the center of my heart. Reaching out to the Exir was the most difficult part. An intricate process that required tremendous strength.

I hadn't anticipated the danger my heightened senses would bring. Every violent heartbeat, every burst of the lush crescendo of every succulent pulsation of Scarlett's heart was distracting. Deafening. A reminder of her humanity, of what the Exir desired the most.

As my Exir began to stir, I was increasingly vulnerable to the *Forbidden*. It wasn't my Nherum form that craved the *Forbidden*. It was the Exir. The most incredible wave of urge swallowed up every sense, every principle, every belief, and everything else that I was. No longer capable of thinking about anything else, I was overwhelmed by the possibility of having a taste of the *one true sublimity*.

My Exir grew stronger with the grave hunger. An intense compulsion pulled me closer to the human standing in front of me, urging me to commit the *Forbidden*. I tried to fight it, but Scarlett didn't make it easy. An agonizing thirst burnt through my Exir as I felt her move toward me. I could taste my euphoria with every step she took. I was ready to succumb to my new purpose. I was ready to give up everything. I was ready to commit the *Forbidden*.

Until warm fingers throbbed against my skin.

Somehow, she gave me the strength to resist. The urge was still strong within me, but I was restrained.

The warmth of her touch still lingered on my face when I heard her speak, "Are you okay, Petyr?" The familiar sound sent me straight back to my senses, and the urge for the *Forbidden* melted in an instant.

I didn't open my eyes. I couldn't look at her knowing what I so desperately wanted to do to her. I wished I had the strength to repel the temptation of the *Forbidden* on my own, but I was grateful for her power to control me, to tame me. This was the moment when I realized I'd always be weak, and I'd always be unworthy. I'd always need her.

The serenity and strength that Scarlett's touch had sparked within me penetrated my Exir. Its essence slithered through my veins until its familiar heat filled my body. I felt the warm light of my Exir as it peered through every pore of my skin. I lifted my arms, extended them to my sides, and waited to be enveloped by the crimson light.

My Exir flourished into its own unique shape, spreading its luminous wings. It was seeping out of my body, claiming liberation, yet it was me. I saw through its eyes, and I felt its radiant wings flutter and sway with the wind. It soared high across the skies, up to the heavens where I truly belonged.

I could hear the others calling. I could feel the attraction luring me to different directions. But I swerved downward to find Scarlett looking up at me. I rushed back down, letting the crimson radiance gradually recede back to the center of my heart.

Scarlett took a deep breath and tried to move her lips a couple of times, but she was unable utter a word.

"Are you scared?" I asked, hoping that this time, it would be my voice that would save her from paralysis.

"I'm dreaming," she finally replied.

"Do you wish it's all a dream?"

"I wish to never wake up." She took a step closer, placed her arms around my neck, and touched my lips with hers. That was the moment I felt incredibly *lucky*.

It was against all the odds that someone like me could ever experience the power, the immense happiness from this abstract notion the humans called love. And for a human, whom by nature embraced ignorance, to witness what I was and still look at me with such affection was beyond improbable.

I took her affection, wrapped my hands around her waist, pulled her even closer, and indulged in the magnetism of her lips. I relished everything luck had brought to me, knowing I deserved none of it. Would she still look at me in the same way if she knew what I was determined to do to her just minutes before?

She needed to know that every time she was with me, she was in danger.

I knew it was only a matter of time before I became, once again, vulnerable to the *Forbidden*. I was aware of the possibility that the urge would become stronger. Neither her presence nor her voice would be enough to bring me back to my senses. If the time came, I knew exactly what would happen.

I would kill her. Then, it would kill me.

Right now, she was my strength. Her warm presence kept me in control of my senses.

"There is something I need to tell you." My words formed in a tentative whisper.

"There is *everything* you need to tell me," she whispered back, but her tone had no trace of apprehension.

"Yes, there is. Let's start with this one." I tried to speak the words louder, in spite of my depleting confidence.

"Go on."

I looked straight into her eyes, hoping somewhere deep in it I'd find a way to make this easier. I had waited so long to have the opportunity to be completely honest with her. "I . . ." I started, reminding myself that she deserved to know everything about me. Including the monster I could be—and what I could do to her. "I will always need you."

Coward.

She smiled. In this moment, it seemed impossible I could ever hurt her. *Maybe the love I have for her is stronger than any dark urge*, I thought, allowing myself to feel a sense of hope.

"You must be freezing. Come on, let's keep you warm," I managed to say when I was certain that I wasn't strong enough to tell her what I needed to, at least not this time.

"I'm fine," she said as she pulled on her coat.

I led her to the space between the roots of a tree nearby.

"Is this supposed to shelter us from the cold?" Her smile told me she knew I had a plan. I returned her smile, took my shirt off, and laid it on the ground for her to sit on.

"I think it's safe to say you don't have to worry about the cold." She snickered as she sat next to me.

"My physical body warms or cools itself as necessary.

Come on, I think you could do with some warmth." I placed an arm on her shoulders.

"Physical," she repeated my word as if it was an unusual term.

"What about it?" I asked.

"You say that like it's not you, like this is not you." She squeezed my hand.

"What you see, what you feel, it's me, of course it's me, but as you have seen, I'm not entirely just this."

"Tell me more."

I felt her shiver.

"Not until I'm sure you're warm enough." The crimson light seeped out of my pores. With a human so close to me, connecting with my Exir was much easier. Her presence attracted it. There was something about the humans that made it unstable, but in this moment, at least, I knew I wasn't about to lose control.

"You're glowing again, are you going to turn . . ." She let her sentence fade, perhaps unsure of how to describe exactly what I turned into.

"No, this is just to keep you warm."

"What do you mean? What is *this*?" She placed her palm over my skin, hovering just above the light radiating from my arm.

"It's called an Exir. It's what you'd probably refer to as a soul."

"It's beautiful." She paused for a few seconds, keeping her gaze on her fingers that traced the surface of my Exir. "What are you?"

"I'm an Empyr. I came from a world called Empyrian."

"Is that another planet?"

"No, it's right here on Earth, just a different realm from the one that you know," I explained.

"This light that glows around you," she continued, ignoring my unhelpful response, "If it's your soul, then it's who you are, right? When you turned, you were luminous, and every time you moved there were sparks, like fireworks, like deep red burning sunset. It was mesmerizing, aggressive but calm, beautiful. Was that you as an Empyr?"

"Not all the time."

"You're really not very good at clarifying things," she sighed. "I mean, in your world, do you still look like this?"

I always found her impatience pleasing. It showed she didn't like wasting time. "When I'm in my Nherum form, yes."

"So you look normal, even when you're in Empyrian?"

"Normal." I knew what she meant, but the word made me laugh. "I have to live with my physical body until my Exir is strong enough to liberate itself. We call it our Nherum form."

"Do you mean you live until you die and your soul leaves your body so it can live forever? That's not so different from being a human, you know."

"I suppose when you put it that way," I agreed, "but there is no fear or uncertainty about the death of our Nherum form. Our physical bodies look like yours, but we're not quite as vulnerable. We don't get diseases, and we can move and think fast enough to eliminate all possible accidents."

"You just wait until your Exir is ready to move on? What happens to your body then?"

"I suppose it just disintegrates. Its only purpose is to hold the Exir until it's strong enough to live without a vessel." I took her hand and placed it on my chest. "Right here, in the core of the heart, is my Exir. It's almost impenetrable."

"That massive, radiant creature can't possibly fit in your heart. And where? Is your heart hollow inside or something?"

I reached out to brush her warm cheeks with the tip of my fingers. "I wish it was easier for you to know me, and you didn't have to go out of your way—"

She took my hand in hers. "There you go again. Stop feeling sorry for me. Stop being afraid for me. I might be physically fragile compared to you, but I'm not weak." She spoke with the confidence she urged me to see in her. "Even if we grew up on the same street and went to the same corner shop every morning, there would always be something to learn about the other person. The only problem is you're so extraordinary, you'll have to answer far more questions."

"I'll try to give you the answers you need," I promised, knowing there was still so much I wasn't willing to confess.

She paused for a few moments. Her breathing had slowed down. I could tell she was deep in thought. "What's wrong?"

"When you were talking about your Exir, you said it was almost impenetrable. Almost. What happens if it breaks?"

"It wouldn't." I fought to push the image of Alex's shattered Exir into the back of my mind.

"So you live until your Exir is ready." Though she looked at me as she spoke, her words seemed to be directed at herself, perhaps still trying to organize her own thoughts.

"Yes, I wait," I replied.

"For how long?"

"For as long as it takes." I found her increasing apprehension due to my temporary physical form rather ironic, considering the vulnerability of her own fleeting existence.

"How long have you been waiting?"

"I think you should take some time to process everything before I give you any more details," I suggested, hoping she would let this one go.

"Tell me," she demanded.

I knew the answer to this question could impair the remarkable way she'd accepted everything I revealed so far. I sighed and spoke the syllables that could finally rouse her to question the plausibility of our relationship. "In your time, five centuries and twenty-seven years."

A deep, thoughtful silence followed my confession. I'd give anything to know what was going through her head.

"You don't grow old," she finally said. It wasn't a question, but I seized the opportunity to explain.

"I do, only much slower than you. My body is designed to last for centuries, for as long as my Exir needs it." My explanation didn't help. She went silent once again. I tried to emphasize the simplicity of the process. I told her about my ability to govern every part of my body and delay the deterioration of my organs. Controlling the course of my aging wasn't more complicated than her ability to mechanically control a muscle. But there was no response.

I decided not to push her. Fear edged my senses as I watched her struggle to comprehend and accept something that wasn't even the worst part of what I was.

She shook her head, as if to shake off her thoughts about my age, and asked, "Are you the only one here?"

I wasn't surprised by her decision to change the topic. I'd have liked to know exactly how she felt, but I understood why this was something she'd rather not think about. I'd tried to do the same thing.

We were locked in different time frames. Different worlds could be crossed, but time was an absolute separation. Her time was brief, and she had no control over it. It would swiftly push her along its limited compass. If she were lucky enough to surpass the countless possibilities of an untimely end, she would grow old and frail. I'd watch the beautiful being that had become the most important part of me crumble and fade. Whilst I remained untouched by time, every piece that completed her would disintegrate.

It would be inevitable. She would be stolen from me, and it would tear me apart. Then, I'd have to carry on with a lifetime of waiting for a ceaseless existence of emptiness.

This thought, this truth, it highlighted the distance between us. We lived in different timeframes. A reminder that, even right now, we didn't share the same moments. We could never truly be together. I understood why Scarlett would rather not think about it. I had tried to push the same thought deep in the back of my mind. I knew that if I didn't, it would lead me to resent my purpose. In fact, it could do more than that. The dangerous thought could drive me to consider the possibility of never having to live without her.

There was a way.

No Empyr would ever choose to do it, but it was possible. I could do it. All I had to do was commit to the choice. There would be grave consequences. It would be the deepest betrayal to my kind, an abomination, a far greater sin than the *Forbidden* . . . but I'd be willing. *If it meant a lifetime with Scarlett, in a heartbeat, I'd be willing.*

I shook the thought out of my mind before it could linger long enough for the others to feel the magnitude of my desire. I shouldn't have allowed myself to pursue this thought in the first place. After all, I didn't have to think about it for now. There was so much more to consider. So much more Scarlett had to know about me. So much more I wasn't sure if I'd ever be brave enough to tell her.

I cleared my throat and tried to focus on the questions I could answer. "No, I live with three others, but we're not all the same."

"How do you mean?"

"We're all from the same world, but of different Corta." Scarlett's eyes narrowed at hearing the unfamiliar word, so I continued before she could ask. "Corta is quite similar to what you call race, but slightly more complicated."

"I think I'm getting better with complicated." The natural exuberance of her voice seemed to be returning gradually.

"You're exceptional." If only my voice could carry the extent of my gratefulness for her patience, for her resilience. "The characters of our Exir are classed in three different Cortas—Astra, Arca, and Agua. Essentially, it defines our abilities. For instance, the way I jumped with you—"

"Jump," she interrupted with a soft chuckle. "Now that's an understatement."

"Or maybe you use the word a little too lightly, seeing that humans can't really jump," I said, returning her tone. "And only a specific type of Empyr can. We're called Astra."

"Astra," she repeated approvingly. "If the others can't jump like you can, what can they do?"

There wasn't enough time to go through every single aspect of each Corta, so I tried to be brief in my descriptions. "In a more general sense, the Arca is the strongest and the fastest kind, especially when they are in physical contact with soil. They can hear the trees, read the land, speak to animals, and . . ." I almost stumbled as memories of how Dru endured Alex's pain resurfaced. "They share their physical and emotional feelings with nature."

"That sounds incredible."

"Yes, their Corta is also known for their compassion," I stated as I thought of Dru's support in understanding my relationship with Scarlett. "They can be dangerous, though. They have another known ability. They called it *Shadowing*. It's a way to deceive and disorient their target."

"How does it work?"

"I'm not entirely sure. The Cortas don't usually share specific details about their significant abilities."

"You have secrets from the other Cortas too?"

"Plenty." I smiled.

"Such as?"

"Let me tell you about the Agua first," I said in an attempt to delay the moment I'd have to focus on telling her about myself. I had been waiting for the chance to finally be honest with her, but even now, I wasn't sure if I could tell her everything.

"You're lucky I'm really interested to know what an Agua is, but you'll have to talk about yourself sooner or later."

"The Agua is less compassionate than the Arca," I said with an almost automatic sneer. I felt Scarlett flinch at the words *merciless* and *cruel*, so I swiftly moved on to their technical abilities. "They have control over water, and they can feel imminent danger. They can also push their thoughts into the minds of others."

"Like mind control?" she asked, visibly impressed.

"No, not like mind control. They can't make you do things, but they can make you hear their voice in your head, so you have no choice but to listen. It's one of the many ways they try to impose their authority on others."

"They have authority over the other Cortas?"

"They'd like to think so."

"But?"

"Well, as I mentioned, each Corta has many abilities they don't disclose to the others. There's no way of knowing who has more power. It's something the ancient leaders of our world agreed on to ensure that peace, or at least order, is kept within our world."

"That makes sense. You wouldn't start a fight if you have no idea what you're up against."

"Exactly." I knew we were getting closer to the time when she'd ask the difficult questions about me.

"So what's it like when an Agua pushes thoughts in your mind? Does it hurt?"

"It's harmless to me, but it can torment the weaker minds, particularly that of a Spark." Spark. As soon as I uttered the word, I regretted it. Scarlett didn't have to know about the Sparks, the living reminders of the flaws of our kind. My resentment towards Sparks grew even stronger because I knew sooner or later Nero would urge me to seek the help of the Spark, Evan, to find treatment for the current state of my emotions. As an Astra, as an Eltor, I couldn't accept I'd ever be in a situation where I'd need the help of a Spark.

Pride wasn't the only reason I clung on to the belief that I didn't need help. This condition, my love for a human, however my kind chose to perceive it, was now a part of me. Not a problem to be solved, and certainly not an ailment to be cured.

I tried to answer Scarlett's question in one swift sentence. "A Spark is an Empyr with a weak Exir." It was sufficient. Scarlett's interest was now completely focused on me, and my ability.

"So you're an Astra," she started. "What's it like?"

"The best." I winked at her before I continued with more useful details. "We have a deep understanding of the heavens and the space beyond. We can read the stars and celestial bodies. We also have a connection with wind."

"Huh." She paused in apparent astonishment. "I always knew you were extraordinary. I guess now I have a better idea of just how much. Tell me more. What else can you do?"

I grinned at the combination of impatience and excitement in her voice. "Let's see, our brains can process information at a maximum speed. For instance, we can analyze every detail in situations, interactions. We compose ourselves, choose the most precise words, gestures, emotions, and posture before the other person can even blink. A strong Astra is supposed to be *all knowing* of the past, future, and everything in between. I used to think I had all the answers. Then, I stumbled upon you"—I laughed—"then I never seemed to stop stumbling."

She didn't return my laughter, and was thoughtful for a few seconds before she spoke. "You're like a god. You know everything."

"Not everything." Not anymore.

She ignored my correction. "Your brain must be so powerful. No one could really know what you're thinking. I wonder how long it'll take you to get bored of constantly overpowering my inferior human brain."

"You have no idea how much you constantly overpower me." I sighed at the reminder of the impact her presence had on me. Not a sigh of defeat, but of acceptance, of gratification.

"At some point you'll see just how insignificant I am." Her voice slightly trembled.

"Don't call yourself insignificant," I demanded earnestly. "You look at me, and instantly I lose control of my senses. You weaken me. You control me." I laughed at how ludicrous the words sounded coming from an Astra. "You probably have no idea just how impossible that sounds." I paused and pressed my hand onto hers. "But you also give me serenity. You save me from my own unforgiving oblivion. You make me weak but, Scarlett Harington, you are my strength. That probably doesn't make a whole lot of sense right now, but someday you'll understand just what you mean to me. For now, don't call yourself insignificant."

She returned the pressure on my fingers. Something told me that somehow she understood.

"I'll try to tone down the paralyzing charm," she finally said in my favorite buoyant tone.

"Please don't. I wouldn't know how to live without it now," I replied through a grin.

"Tell me about your world, Em . . ."

"Empyrian."

"Yes, Empyrian. Where is it exactly? How can it be on Earth and not have been discovered by humans?"

"The Earth, the universe even, it's a lot bigger than humans think. You only see what you know, and that's just a minute part of it. Your senses aren't equipped to see the rest. For example, you think the space around the planets is just vast darkness, but it's not. Your eyes are just not strong enough to see how vibrant it is, full of life and worlds and incredible places."

"This is crazy," she said, shaking her head. "You know, there was a time when I was younger. I was looking at an ant, and I had this thought. I wondered if it had any idea how big the world was. Right now, I feel like I'm that ant. I haven't even seen our world for what it really is, and you're telling me that there are loads of other worlds out there? Have you been to many?"

"Yes, part of what an Astra does is to discover and explore different worlds. The region of Empyrian where I live, it's high up, so high that our view of the space and the worlds above is not obscured by clouds."

"I'm guessing you have no need for space suits. It's probably safe to say that it would be somewhat inconvenient for me to visit your house." She delivered her words with playful banter, but I felt the sting of the reminder that she would never be able to see my world. "How do you get to Empyrian anyway?"

"There were times when I've dreamt of having this conversation with you, so I've actually thought about how I would explain this one. You have stories in your literature that I think will help you understand. Think of Wonderland or Narnia or Neverland or stories about Fairies."

She laughed.

"I sound ridiculous I know, but those concepts may help you put it in perspective. My home is on Earth, but different space, different concept of time, different world. If you're in the right place, you can literally jump into my world."

"Maybe one day you can show me where that wardrobe is, but only if you promise I can have some pixie dust," she teased. "So what brought you to my humble world?"

The grin faded from my face. This was the moment that could liberate me. This was also the moment that could make Scarlett turn her back on me.

"To learn," I replied cautiously, and continued before she could ask more questions about my purpose in the human world. "I think it's time you got some rest. You have a lot to process. Everything else can wait. Let me take you home." I cringed at my own cowardice. I wasn't brave enough to tell her about the *Forbidden*. I wasn't sure I'd ever be.

"Just a couple more minutes," she said, closing her eyes as she leaned close to me. I let myself revel in the euphoria of her presence. My face was buried in her soft hair, drinking in her exquisite scent and listening to the entrancing rhythm of her heartbeat. But there was no danger, just an immense sense of belongingness and serenity, perpetual serenity.

"I feel like you're going to disappear." Her voice was soft, almost as if she were not intending for me to hear her words.

"I'm right here, where my heart is," I whispered.

VI. SHADOWING

I had turned my back on Scarlett.

There was nothing else to do but jump, without looking back. But no matter how hard I pushed, it wasn't enough to mend the burning hole in my heart.

With the way Scarlett so effortlessly accepted me, I almost had myself fooled. I almost believed we could stay together despite the odds.

From the moment I confessed everything, I spent as much time as I could with her. She jumped with me, and each time, she grew less and less apprehensive. When I showed her my dwelling space, she didn't recoil at my flagrant disconformity from the conventional living structure of a human home. In fact, much like everything else I showed her about myself, she embraced the very aspects that made it different.

"This place is amazing," she exclaimed when she first stepped into my apartment. "Look at all this space. I should really get rid of some of the clutter in my room." Her voice echoed in my mind, the candid buoyancy still crisp in my memory.

The way she handled Nero's intrusive questions and Kara's offensive remarks was even more impressive. Dru had been helpful in shifting her attention away from the other two, but Scarlett didn't need any help. Scarlett's answer to Nero's invasive questions would often include unnecessary intimate details that left him feeling uncomfortable. There was no hint of antagonism or defensiveness in her responses. She retained the usual sparkle in her voice when she spoke to Nero. Though there was always a hint of subtle mockery that she didn't necessarily intend to conceal.

Even with this dark emptiness in my chest, I could almost laugh as I pictured Scarlett's mischievous eyes locked into mine, conveying triumph over Nero's attempt to scrutinize her. I did warn her of what to expect from the others, but no warning could have given anyone that much coolness and craft. No, it was all Scarlett.

From my place, we made our way to Dru's. "I swear my local gym doesn't have this much stuff," she jested. It had also been converted into one room, occupied by the treadmill, cycling, rowing, and ski machines. Dru relied on these things to keep him physically engaged as he passed time during the nights.

Kara's place, on the other hand, had a slightly different structure. It was divided into two floors. "Must you really show her my space?"

"I'm trying to give her an idea of who we are," I replied.

"It's your decision to show her who you are. She doesn't need to know who I am." Her voice didn't carry any hostility, but there was a hint of defensiveness.

"We might be of different Cortas, but we're both Empyr. You're part of who I am," I reasoned, allowing sincerity to touch the surface of my factual statement.

Kara didn't respond. She turned her back and led the way. The first floor gave the impression of walking into a grand closet. The clothes were organized by color. There were spaces for shoes and bags, various musical instruments, priceless antiques, and paintings. In the middle of her elaborately decorated room was a king-size bed with a golden frame, which matched the golden tub in her equally elaborate bathroom. On the second floor, a glass water tank took up most of the room. Aquariums filled with a variety of fish covered each wall.

"What do you think?" I asked Scarlett, wondering if she could get a sense of Kara's nature.

"I think"—she paused for a moment as she glanced at Kara—"I think Kara has incredible taste."

I could tell Scarlett had so many questions, but she also knew it wasn't the time to ask, considering Kara had enough reservations about letting her see the place.

Nero's apartment was the only one that hadn't been structurally altered. He kept all the original wall divisions and the ceilings; he had a dining room, a bedroom, and even guest rooms. His place looked like a normal human house. Even though Nero would have been more comfortable living in my apartment, he believed living exactly as a human wouldn't only make it easier for him to get used to behaving like one, but also aid his understanding of them.

When we reached the shared apartment, I realized I didn't feel as protective of Scarlett as I thought I'd be. I didn't need to defend her, even with Kara's deliberate incivility.

Her humanity was a constant reminder of her vulnerability against my race. Yet, she stood in front of the others, aware of their physical and mental superiority, but without a single trace of intimidation. In that room, it was all too obvious, she had an innate strength within her. She was fearless. She was so feeble, so delicate, but so strong.

That strength didn't fade when it was time for me to leave her. Fighting to speak through a stream of unremitting tears, she demanded me to keep my word. "You promised you wouldn't leave. When you told me what you were, you promised you'd stay here, with me."

Her voice reverberated in my mind, over and over again, and every syllable struck me with a lightning of pain more unbearable than the last.

She stood in front of me, urging me to keep my promise—that I'd always be there. But I was unable to speak. The only thing I wanted to say was that I'd stay, but it wasn't an option.

I'd have said that everything was going to be all right, and no matter what happened, I'd find my way back to her.

If I could speak, if there was no violent fire in my throat, if there was no searing rock rested against my chest, burning an agonizing hole though my heart, I'd have said something—anything—to reduce her pain.

But I left her. The hole in my chest blazed at the memory of Scarlett's wounded eyes staring into mine, pleading.

The heavens darkened. The wind that was enveloping me with its warm solace had now retreated from my cold skin. An unfamiliar sensation of a sharp blade forcing open an exhausted wound stung my core and burnt my eyes. Each time my feet touched the ground I wanted to turn back. Just one slight tilt, and I could be making my way back to Scarlett.

But I was bound to return to Empyrian.

I had to keep going, and a compelling force of frozen mist and hailstone surging close beside me made sure I did.

I'd jumped alone for over five centuries. But ever since Scarlett came into my life, I'd almost forgotten how to be alone. She offered me a place in her human life. She took me to her favorite places and introduced me to the people she referred to as family and friends. She had become the bridge that connected me to a new understanding of her world. Because of her, there were times when I no longer felt like an outsider.

Somehow, I still felt that connection. Even as I rushed away—as I kicked the fierce wind, commanding height and distance from the place I was now compelled to leave—I still felt like I belonged here.

As an Empyr, as an Astra born to lead my kind, I should have known exactly what was going to happen. I should have found a way to prevent it. Even on that innocent day, when the wind was harsh, but the sunlight fought through the royal sky, I should have known. I should have fought harder when I sensed the concealed entity—vigilant, patient, like a predator waiting for the exact moment to reveal itself to its oblivious prey. But I wasn't oblivious, and I was certainly not prey.

I was simply—distracted.

Scarlett could barely contain the excitement in her eyes when she led me to the isolated lake. "It's beautiful, isn't it?"

"It is." I nodded in agreement. There was nothing particularly remarkable about the place. The misty grass was overgrown. Moss polluted the iced lake. Brown leaves covered the muddy ground. A picture of neglect, but somehow, with the stillness of it all, I could see the beauty Scarlett meant.

"And look," she exclaimed, pointing to a thick branch of the tallest tree in the secluded meadow. On the branch was what looked like a small wooden shelter. A flat, rectangular piece of wood was attached on the branch, like a bench. On either side was two narrow but thicker pieces of wood, supporting a plastic roofing.

"That's been there for as long as I can remember," Scarlett explained.

Though I had come to the same conclusion—at the sight of the plastic roof smeared by the memories of rain and harsh sunlight, and the wood tainted with dirt and age—I nodded silently without interrupting her train of thought.

"My dad used to take me out here to ride my bike, and I remember looking up there feeling annoyed because it was too high. I was certain when I grew up I'd magically have the skills to climb up there." She shook her head and let out a self-conscious laugh.

The wooden shelter was on the highest branch. Though not impossible, there was certainly more danger than benefit in climbing the tree to get to the framed branch. Who would place a resting area on such a curious place? There was a sudden ripple of excitement in my brain as it acknowledged the mystery. I'd have pursued it if only I wasn't more interested in distracting Scarlett. She was clearly concerned that the irrationality of her childish thought would highlight the inferiority of her mind. Perhaps it was my growing connection to humanity, but I didn't think believing that someday she'd have the ability to touch something out of reach was absurd.

"Maybe it's time we made magic happen," I suggested. I took off my coat, an item that would serve a purpose other than another layer to my costume. I pulled Scarlett into my free arm and pushed us up to the wooden shelter. I laid my coat on the unkempt surface of the wood, placed Scarlett on it, and took my place beside her.

"You have got to stop doing that," she complained with slow emphasis on each word. She tried to hold a disapproving look that barely concealed the smile in the corner of her lips.

"I know. I should act like a gentleman and ask for your permission before sweeping you off your feet," I replied through a grin as I placed a hand on her shoulder. "But I don't think I can afford to miss that expression on your face."

"Ha. This? This is pure irritation and frustration and—"

"And maybe just a hint of enjoyment?"

"Will you ever tone down that super brain, picking up every hint of every damn thing?"

"Will you ever tone down that merciless charm, leaving my super brain erratic every damn time?"

"Well I guess we both have a problem." Her eyes locked onto mine, releasing the invisible shackles that still never ceased to capture me. She leaned forward, touched her lips on mine for one fleeting second, and then she pulled away. "That's all you're getting, for being cheeky."

"You cruel thing," I groaned as I craved the taste of her lips and the feel of her skin against mine.

"How can I be cruel? I brought you here," she declared with a rather animated gesture.

"That's true," I agreed with an exaggerated buoyancy to match hers, hoping to cover up the physical tension that still lingered in the air.

"I know it's not the prettiest place in the world, and you won't get to be as high as you'd prefer, but it's peaceful. No one ever comes here anymore. Even in the summer, everyone goes to the park on the other side of town."

"But you used to come here?" Something about this curious place didn't quite add up.

"Yeah, a long time ago though. A lot of people used to come here for picnics and bike rides and to feed the ducks. I wonder whatever happened to those ducks. Now this place just seems so out of the way." A thought gleamed in my mind for a fraction of a second—*the place was forgotten for a reason*—but was pushed away by a more pressing concern.

A noise.

The part of my brain that monitored our surroundings detected a clear, unmistakable sound of movement that revealed the identity of our intruder. It was the slight brush of a bare foot on the dry edge of a leaf, careful not to crush the dead piece of plant—an Arca.

The sound was inaudible to Scarlett, so I turned to warn her before I moved. "We have company." Before she could respond, I placed my hands around her waist and pushed us off the tree. My feet landed, but I held her a few inches off the ground for a full second to let her catch her breath before I placed her down. Almost driven by a reflex, I took a step forward and held an arm in front of her.

"We both know what you need to do now," I addressed our intruder without having to raise my voice to be heard.

Though careful, there was no hesitation in the footsteps. The breathing was controlled, yet calm. No sign of aggression. No physical threat. But of course, there was always danger. As long as I was with Scarlett, she would always be in danger. If I wasn't even certain I could protect her from myself, then how was I supposed to ensure her safety from all the other threats my poor decisions had pulled out of my world, into hers? An Arca approached, capable of *Shadowing*, of distorting my perception. I shuddered at the thought of the damage it could do to Scarlett's mind. I glanced at Scarlett's tense face, but I detected no fear in her eyes. I almost wanted to smile. This girl wasn't afraid of anything.

But I was afraid. They knew about her. I wanted to jump, to get her to a safe place where all the dangers attached to me would never reach her. But there was no such place, not now, not with me.

The precise footsteps picked up speed. In a split second, there she was, standing just a few paces in front of us.

"Leera," I heard myself whisper.

"Petyr"—she flashed a measured smile and continued— "you really needed to be alone for this." The calmness in her tone wasn't enough to cover up the sense of urgency. Whatever it was that made her travel to the human realm, she would have to tell me right here, in front Scarlett.

"This is not real," I affirmed, observing her immaculate form. My gaze scrutinized the uncharacteristic sleekness of her long, black hair that wasn't the least bit windblown from running. Pristine, white dress elegantly draped her composed posture. Her eyes met mine with an uncharacteristic, controlled detachment.

She let out a childish laugh that didn't match her current appearance. "Of course it's not real. Would you have expected me to wander around the human world in my real Nherum form? Petyr, it seems you're as defected as they said you'd be." Her final words were not scornful, but worse— edged with pity.

"I know why you're here." I spoke with cold certainty. An attempt to prove I was still the same Astra, able to perceive and comprehend anything infinitely faster than any other Corta.

"Are you sure about that?" she asked with forced mockery.

Arcas were never good at hiding their sentiments. Though I could see her anxiety and concern, I couldn't tolerate her persistent insolence to doubt my abilities.

I started with an intentional detachment to emphasize my authority. "Leera, you came here to tell me they know about the human." I struggled to hold my posture for a fraction of a moment—though not long enough for Leera to notice—as my reflexes recoiled in disgust with the way I referred to Scarlett. *The human.* That was all Scarlett was to them. The insignificant creature that distracted the great Empyr from a critical mission. The inconvenience.

"They know so much more than—"

"They felt my close encounter with the *Forbidden*," I said, interrupting her attempt to once again challenge my ability. "But I'm still here, and so is my Exir." I was still here because of Scarlett and how I felt about her, but Leera didn't have to know that.

"This is not about that."

"The ruthless power of the *Forbidden* has burnt through my veins, yet I stand before you, untouched by the supposed greatest weakness of our kind."

Scarlett was listening intently to my every word. I knew she would ask about the *Forbidden*, and I had no idea what I'd say to her. How would I tell her about the inherent flaw that could so easily drive me to take both our lives? How would I tell her without losing her?

I'd have to lie.

I'd always been skilled when it came to deceit. I was an Astra, after all. I knew too many truths, and if I told the truth every time someone asked for it, there would be chaos. However, lying to Scarlett was the most difficult. I thought telling her my true identity would ultimately allow me to be completely honest, but I could never seem to find the strength to tell her about the *Forbidden*.

The lie I had to conjure up for Leera wasn't much easier. All I had to do was pretend I, alone, was powerful enough to save myself from the *Forbidden*. It was shameful. The lie covered up my weakness, but with it was Scarlett's strength.

There was one more reason for Leera's decision to enter the human world, perhaps the most important one. My subsequent words were vital. I owed Scarlett so much.

Even if I told her about the *Forbidden*, even if it scared her away, it would always be my flaw, my burden to take. But I knew that the fundamental reason why Leera was here was something Scarlett would claim as her fault.

The night I revealed my identity to Scarlett, I allowed myself to think of—and commit to—the only possible way I wouldn't have to live without her. The thought in itself was a deplorable betrayal to my kind. Scarlett would blame herself. It would be difficult to make her believe that this betrayal would be my own selfish act. If I ever had the strength to go through with it, I'd be doing it to save myself from centuries of desolation.

I chose my words carefully when I continued. "If I can regain control despite the force of the *Forbidden*, then I haven't, nor will I ever fall. I entertained the thought of a mere possibility a fraction longer than I should have. That is my only sin. It was a single thought, not an act."

"It's a thought no Empyr should have."

"I have an infinite amount of thoughts, Leera. I'm an Astra. I hold everything in my mind, but of course I can't expect you to comprehend that."

It wasn't in my nature to inflict offense. My brain was far too rational for that. I also knew very well that an Arca's inability to understand how my mind worked was no more than my limited knowledge of *Shadowing*. Still, I spoke like an Agua, imposing superiority. A part of me did want Leera to feel inferior for the way her presence had forced me to refer to Scarlett as one.

"I'm an Eltor just as much as you are." She flashed a cold smile and continued, "You know I'm on your side."

"Does it make complete sense that you'd travel all that way just to express your concern? Could it have something to do with a curious appetite for the sight of a fallen Astra?"

The subtle changes in Leera's expression were swift and guarded—from her surprise at the bluntness of my statement, to her shame at the apparent truth in it, to a thoughtful pause until the cold smile returned. Then her eyes left me and found Scarlett. "I don't think the bitter air suits him, do you?"

This was the first time Leera acknowledged Scarlett. I inched closer to her, barely managing to control my reflexes. I wanted to shield her from the source of the building anxiety that impelled her heartbeat. Leera's presence made Scarlett uneasy in a way that neither Nero nor Kara ever had. I wondered if she could sense that unlike the others, Leera was young, inexperienced, and impulsive with neither the desire nor the responsibility to tolerate humans. Yet Scarlett, being Scarlett, held herself with such tenacity. Her eyes were fixed on Leera's, but she seemed unwilling to respond. I could tell she wanted to show Leera she wasn't intimidated, and she was definitely not afraid. I was too proud of her to point out the dangers of this irrational bravery.

Leera's eyes didn't leave Scarlett's as she addressed me. "I can see why you find this one so appealing. It's not often you find something so out of place, so difficult to read."

She'd also realized there was something different about Scarlett. If I gave her the chance to figure out just how much of Scarlett I couldn't comprehend, she would easily see the difference in me. She would see through my thin veneer of composure and find my erratic condition. She would find what she came to see: a fallen Astra.

I had to move her attention away from Scarlett, and there was only one question left to ask. "Are they sending Aris?"

Being an Astra, having to ask questions would always feel unnatural. Scarlett was the only enigma I could tolerate. I was always the one with the answers, and I did have an answer this time. Still, I needed to ask and hope Leera would provide a different answer. There was a glimmer of dread on Leera's face that she couldn't attempt to conceal. Cautious not to meet my eyes, she confirmed with a single sharp nod. Hope had failed me this time. Aris was coming.

Aris was an Aguan Eltor, infamous for his merciless and fierce disposition. The Supreme Eltors, the most superior beings of Empyrian, would never risk allowing Aris to enter the human world. Not unless they thought it was absolutely necessary.

Everything was clear. I'd tried to deny it. Now, I must accept it. My kind had lost faith in me. They believed I had betrayed them. The night I confessed my identity to Scarlett, in one careless moment, I allowed myself to consider the possibility of never having to live a life without her. The possibility of an alternative life—*as human*. They felt my certainty. They knew it was more than just a thought. It was a decision.

Aris, who refused to see the value of any Empyr that wasn't an Agua, was a fundamental threat to humans. At this point, our mission in this world was no longer the priority. All that mattered now was the restoration of my allegiance, and there was only one obvious way to do this: eliminate the distraction.

Eliminate Scarlett.

A sharp pain stabbed through the core of my heart at the realization of the great danger I had placed her in. I should have seen this coming. The Astra I was would never have been so reckless to let this happen. Aris would come for Scarlett, executing any other human who got in his way. I could barely hold my façade in front of Leera. I needed to think, to breathe, to calculate the possibilities. I needed to jump.

I had to figure out a safe place for Scarlett, a place where Aris could never harm her. If he found her, he wouldn't only *kill* her. He would erase her, including her soul. Scarlett would be removed from her world, like she never existed. But I would always remember her. Her captivating gaze, the warmth in her smiles, the traces of her sweet scent, and the echoes of her voice would always linger in my mind. Her memories would be a constant reminder that my incompetence robbed Scarlett of her right to exist.

I ached to reach out and take her in my arms, to keep her

there where I could ensure her safety. But I fought to keep control just long enough for a parting statement. "Thank you, Leera. I think it's time for you to leave."

"I suppose it is." She took a step back, but paused to meet my gaze one last time. "Petyr, you're right about what I came to see, but I'm glad for what I didn't see." Her last few words faded as she disappeared into the trees.

When Leera was out of sight, I moved toward Scarlett and locked her in my arms. Barely managing to breathe, I whispered, "I'm so sorry."

"She seems to know you really well," she said, ignoring my apology.

"That was Leera—"

"Yeah, I caught her name." Scarlett sighed and continued, almost to herself, "She looked incredible."

I knew what she meant. Kara's lustrous hair, Nero's striking eyes and Dru's carved physique used to catch Scarlett's eyes and leave traces of astonishment on her face, but she had grown used to how physically attractive my kind appeared to humans. Leera, however, appeared to us with an immaculate beauty.

"That wasn't her. It wasn't real. Leera is an Arca like Dru. Do you remember what I said about *Shadowing?*"

Scarlett nodded. Though her uncertainty was still evident, I moved on to explain the news Leera had brought with her. "Scarlett, Leera was here for a reason. She came here to—"

"What's an Eltor?" Scarlett asked in a tone that made it clear she no longer wanted to talk about Leera. Without giving me the chance to protest, she continued, "You said you're an Empyr, but that woman, shadow or whatever it was, said she's an Eltor *too*, which means so are you. You're an Empyr, then an Astra, and now you're also something else?"

"Eltor is a rank, a title for the leaders and future leaders of Empyrian."

"You were chosen to be the leader of your world?"

"I was born an Eltor."

"So it's your birthright, like a prince or king or something?"

"Scarlett, we have no time to—" I started to explain that there were more pressing issues to discuss than my status in Empyrian. However, still oblivious to the graveness of our situation, she was determined to pursue her own unanswered questions.

"I need to know this. It's who you are," she insisted.

I sighed and hastened to give her the answers she needed. "I suppose it is similar to your idea of royalty, but it's more than that. Eltors have more power and capabilities than an ordinary Empyr. We have the highest quality of Exir, state of mind, physical strength . . . everything."

"You're the most flawless of your flawless kind?" she said with an uneasy, humorless laugh.

"I suppose you can put it that way. Now listen—" I tried to move on to a more urgent issue, but she wasn't willing to let this one go just yet.

"Huh, just as I start getting used to how extraordinary you are, you turn out to be more. Imagine what your extra-perfect family would say when they find out you've been spending all your time with a ridiculously flawed human." Anxiety became more evident in her voice.

This would have been the time to explain everything and help her understand the situation, but when I looked into her eyes, there was already so much worry. I knew she felt insignificant compared to my supposed superiority. Couldn't she see how much more flawed I was?

"We don't have families like you do. Dru, Nero, and Kara are Eltors, too, so I guess they are my family, and last time I checked, you've already won them over."

I held on to the memory of that moment as I soared closer to Empyrian. I wished I could have stayed there, when I still had her in my arms before I left her broken. I had so many regrets. In that moment, I already knew our fate. There was no future for us. The choices were clear, and I knew that—soon—I'd have to walk away and leave her with a broken heart.

Broken but beating.

But I couldn't break her heart then, not in that moment, not yet.

When she asked what I meant when I said I had *a close encounter with the Forbidden,* I refused to answer. It wasn't just because I was afraid to hurt her, but because I was afraid she would see me for the monster I was. When she insisted on an answer, I stated, "There's no time to explain because we're in danger."

"What danger?" she asked, her voice more curious than alarmed.

"I will explain later. For now I'll take you home. Then I need to go and speak to the others," I said, making sure she heard the strong urgency in my voice. "I will keep you safe. I promise. If it's the last thing I do, I will keep you safe. Don't be scared. I won't let any harm come to you," I added when she didn't respond.

Her voice was steady when she said, "I'm not scared. You should tell me what's going on."

I shook my head and held her close to me, preparing to jump. "There's no time." Though I knew I could spare a few seconds to explain, I needed a reason to avoid all the questions for now.

I kicked the air with the same bitterness as I did now that I could almost see the passage back to Empyrian. I was filled with the same guilt and shame I carried now, but back then, I had no right to dwell on those feelings. Unlike today, I had Scarlett in my arms.

All I could think about was getting to her house as fast as possible, so I could land and leave her there. A part of me knew it would be the last jump. Still, I didn't stop to appreciate the privilege of having her in my arms, so close I could almost taste her scent.

I wanted to be with her. I did. But I had only two

priorities in mind at the time. The first was to save her from something worse than death, and the second was to ensure she didn't discover anything that would lead her to despise me. This was why I refused when she insisted on going to the apartment with me to, in her words, *Help* me *figure things out*. After all, I already knew what was going to happen. There was nothing else to figure out.

I felt a violent twist in my stomach as I remembered the heavy sound of defeat in her sigh, when she said, "Be careful and don't do anything reckless. I'll tell my mum to cancel dinner, but will I see you tomorrow?"

I didn't want her to think about tomorrow. "Don't worry about me."

That was just Scarlett, always thinking about everyone else but herself. I knew she was aware of the cold distance I had managed to conjure up between us, but she chose to understand. She always gave me her complete trust. I knew I didn't deserve it. Because of me, Scarlett's life would change. I'd break her heart and cast a dark cloud of anguish. It would be inevitable, but not yet. There was no reason to cancel our plan and disrupt her life earlier than necessary.

Since we were first invited for dinner at Scarlett's house a few weeks ago—we, meaning Nero, who introduced himself as my brother, and Dru, whom I introduced, more realistically, as my best friend—it became a regular custom.

Though I'd rather not have Nero in my private moments with Scarlett and her family, his presence had actually been rather advantageous. Since he was more skilled in interacting with the humans, the initial uneasiness in the atmosphere faded very quickly. Nero spent most of the evenings either engaged in pleasant conversations with Scarlett's parents, Jon and Helen, or impressing Jack with his magic tricks and fascinating stories, leaving more space for me to spend time with Scarlett. This made his presence considerably tolerable.

It became clear the humans were delighted by Nero's

company, but I was surprised to see how much his relationship with the humans seemed to mean to him. Every time we came for dinner, he brought a piece of gemstone for Jack. He related specific details about the mineral including its compositions and where it came from. Jack listened with attentive ears, often scribbling in a notepad Scarlett had given him after repeatedly insisting he needed an *official book* to document his collections. Jon and Helen naturally assumed Nero was making up the fictional history for the pieces of worthless novelties to entertain Jack. They had no reason to think that within their reach, inside their home, were genuine treasures from another world. From places only Astras with the most powerful Exir could reach, the minerals were rare and coveted even in Empyrian. These could be the greatest discovery of mankind, and even a window to another world.

It was dangerous, and even Dru could see that Nero was breaking some rules, but somehow the gesture didn't *feel* wrong. I could tell Nero wanted the humans to know him, too. This was his way to introduce himself.

Apart from the waves of astonishment that briefly covered his face when Nero described specific details about the objects, Dru didn't do anything to highlight Nero's uncharacteristic insubordination. He seemed to have understood the desire to break free from the pretense and reveal something real, however subtle.

I could tell Dru valued the opportunity to be in such proximity with the humans, to learn and improve his confidence in interacting with them. His discomfort from being in such restricted space, having to stay still for longer than he'd ever needed to, resulted in a sense of awkwardness. Helen interpreted it as being shy, a quality she seemed to find endearing.

I, on the other hand, didn't receive the same warmth quite as easily. Jack had declared his dislike of me the first day I met him, and it took time for him to get used to my presence. After all, unlike Nero, I had nothing interesting to offer him. I had initially gotten a rather similar reception from Scarlett's parents. Though I didn't give them any reason to doubt my intentions, their distrust was only too apparent as they scrutinized my every word and move. However, the more I visited and spent time with them, the more welcoming they became to me.

Partly because I didn't want to disrupt Scarlett's life any sooner than I had to, I asked her not to cancel our plans. "We'll be at dinner. Six o'clock, as usual."

It didn't make a difference. I still had to leave and turn my back on her. As I inched closer to Empyrian, the surrounding air grew thicker, to discourage the humans from approaching.

I was about to enter a realm Scarlett would never reach. I wished I could return to answer all of her questions, but I left without allowing her to know everything about me. I left a coward.

She had every right to hate me. Even though I had broken my promise and left her, she would still see me as a creature who loved her. The one who left only to save her. I should have told her what I really was. She could have had the choice and the reason to feel that hate. I deserved that hate.

She would never know that, more than once, I'd come so close to taking her life.

VII. SEPARATION

The silence was coarse when I entered the shared apartment. Each gaze was fixed on me, carrying an immense ambivalence of judgment, panic, dread, concern, and pity.

No one dared to speak.

They were not waiting for an explanation. They knew. Dru would have felt Leera's presence, Kara would have felt the danger that came with her news, and Nero would have figured out the grave fate I had brought to myself.

They knew everything, which was precisely why there could only be silence. What could they say to someone who had made the decision to betray them?

"When I told her who I was, and she accepted me, I entertained a brief thought. There was nothing more to it." I dared to lie. There was nothing I could say to make them understand why I'd allow myself to entertain the thought of such unforgivable betrayal to our kind, so I attempted to change the focus of their attention. "That same night, I came close to the *Forbidden*. I'd lost myself. I'd surrendered to the act, but Scarlett saved me. She brought me back to my senses. Her presence, her voice, her touch—"

"Your love for her stopped you from committing the *Forbidden*," Dru stated, aiding me to evade the topic of my disloyalty.

"It certainly rendered me incapable of hurting her." I was unwilling to admit the words, *I don't know*. The truth was, I hadn't considered why or how she managed to save me from the *Forbidden*. While it made sense that my love for her would give her the power to tame me, the *Forbidden* wasn't a simple condition or a state of mind that could easily be replaced. It was a compelling force that took over the Exir. At the time, I was no longer myself, I was no longer the creature who loved Scarlett. Still, she managed to bring me back.

"It also rendered you incapable of being the Astra that you are. You were unable to control your thoughts, Petyr, the one ability that defined us. Let us not lose focus of the real predicament, which has little to do with the *Forbidden*. This is about how you allowed a stray thought *commit* you to the betrayal of our kind."

So my lie hadn't fooled Nero. He knew an insignificant thought wouldn't catch the attention of the Supreme Eltors.

"He has not betrayed anyone. Nothing has been done," Dru retorted in my defense. "Pete, just say you won't do it. Just say it and make them believe you."

This was one of the rare times when I envied Dru for being an Arca. His Corta allowed him to perceive nothing much more than the peripheral. He didn't have the Astra's burden of seeing the never-ending strings of complexities. Nothing was ever straightforward. Thoughts and situations were always layered with a myriad of reasons and possibilities.

Nero merely sneered at Dru's naivety for believing that just uttering the words could reverse everything. If only I could simply use my skills as an Astra to augment the sense of sincerity until no one could dispute its authenticity. But this had nothing to do with words or appearances. "You, of all Empyrs, should have known better. The Supreme Eltors won't stop until they are certain you're restored."

Nero's words caught Dru's interest, but I shook my head before he could say something. He seemed to understand. Just as he wouldn't be willing to discuss the full extent of *Shadowing*, certain truths were simply not to be shared across Cortas.

Both Dru and Nero stared at me, puzzled, as I allowed a faint grin to spread from the corner of my lips. I remembered Scarlett's frustration when she learned that not only was I an

Empyr and an Astra, but also an Eltor. What would she say when she found out I was also the *Shield* of Empyrian, carrying power most Empyrs believed to be a myth? My smile faded as I considered how abilities and titles served as invisible barriers between us. The more she discovered, the thicker the barriers became and the further away she seemed from me.

That kind of careless behavior is precisely why you're in this predicament. Kara pushed her words into my mind.

I turned my head, expecting to find her usual dispassionate demeanor. Her deep-blue eyes fixed on me. Intense disapproval marked her expression, but her gaze was soft with pity.

She was right. I allowed the smile to manifest just as I let the unacceptable thought linger in my mind long enough to carry the consequence.

"You're capable." This time she spoke her words.

I shook my head, but not in disagreement. I know I could still be capable of convincing the Supreme Eltors, but that wasn't my only struggle.

Dru threw his hands into the air with a defeated sigh. Kara rarely pushed her words to Dru's mind, claiming it was too inferior for her inner voice. No Empyr appreciated the intrusive echo of an Agua's thoughts, but unlike Nero and me, Dru wasn't always able to grasp threads of thoughts with the absence of certain words. Every time Kara pushed her words to either my mind or Nero's, the other would be able to fill in the gaps and follow the conversation. Dru would always be left excluded.

This time, however, Kara's inner voice didn't have the usual severity of an Agua. It carried the faintest yet unmistakable trace of concern. This wasn't about imposing superiority by being heard, and this was certainly not about a malicious attempt to accentuate Dru's incompetence. I could tell Kara compelled me to listen not for any superficial motive, but for my own benefit. Nevertheless, Dru would never accept Kara to be capable of anything more than malice. Instead of wasting time defending Kara's intentions, I turned to Dru. "How can we make sure no human is harmed by Aris or any other Empyr?" I already knew the answer. Yet, I asked not to simply give Dru the opportunity to contribute, but because I needed to hear the answer from someone I trusted. He was the only one whose opinion wouldn't be tainted by personal agenda.

"We can't," Dru finally said after a few seconds of deliberation. "There is no way we can control them once they're here, so we can't let them come. That means you . . ." He avoided my gaze as he fought and failed to continue.

"I have to go to them." I finished the thought, saving Dru the strain of having to affirm my fate.

"I'm sorry."

"It's not your fault." No, the fault was all mine.

"I will keep her safe, for you," Dru promised, though he still seemed hesitant.

"Thank you, Dru. Knowing you'll be here will make this easier for me," I lied. With Dru's loyalty, physical strength, and speed, I felt confident he'd be able to protect Scarlett, but *nothing* would ever make this easy for me.

I had to cling to hope, now more than ever. I hoped I'd be strong enough to jump away from Scarlett's world without looking back. I hoped, for her sake, I could make the Supreme Eltors believe they hadn't lost the *Shield* of Empyrian.

"You'll need me to go with you," Kara declared.

I shook my head. "I'll be fine." Though I'd inflicted enough certainty in my voice, I knew she wouldn't let the matter go unless she received a rational explanation, so I continued. "It will be more useful if you stay here. You can warn Dru if you sense any danger. It's unlikely once I've spoken to the Supreme Eltors, but I'd rather leave knowing Scarlett has all the protection she can have."

"I'm the only one who can know Aris's moves, which is precisely why you need me. I can tell you exactly where he is, and what he decides to do, as soon as he does. Right now, I can say you have time, but things can very easily change. If Aris decides to leave now, he will be in this world before you reach Empyrian. By the time you realize, it will be too late to turn back and protect the human," Kara asserted.

"That makes sense," Dru admitted, overtly supporting an Agua. He had potentially forfeited his pride for the sake of my affairs. "Don't worry, Pete, she will be safe with me."

Dru had been a true and loyal friend for centuries, and I knew his mind, but for a moment, there was a glimmer in his eyes I didn't recognize. A distinct eagerness, a hunger, to protect the humans. I dismissed the thought after a brief justification that between the times Dru spent helping me analyze Scarlett's effect on my mind and visiting the Haringtons, he had developed a new level of compassion for them.

Nero didn't seem to notice the same glimmer in Dru's eyes. Nonetheless, he threw me an accusing glance for not recognizing that Dru's determination to show loyalty had rendered him oblivious to the consequences of challenging the decision of the Supreme Eltors. If this were the case, Dru would be in a position of great sacrifice with nothing to gain. *He knows what he's doing. Perhaps this is his way of seizing the opportunity to achieve his sense of purpose in this world,* I thought, convincing myself that since Dru had always believed in me, it was now my turn to have faith in him.

Nero didn't care enough about Dru to argue. He simply shrugged and turned to Kara. "You would betray your own Corta?" It wasn't a genuine question, but a way to highlight the flaw in this picture.

Kara flashed a devious smile. "I'm unpredictable." She wasn't about to reveal her real intentions, and Nero didn't expect her to. I could tell he was simply reminding me of how much Corta meant to an Agua. It was much more likely that Kara was working with her superior, Aris, to ensure I returned to Empyrian.

"It doesn't matter, Nero. Ensuring the humans' safety is what's important." An Agua's betrayal was a risk I was willing to take.

"I will have no part in this." His tone was cold. "I condoned your connection with Scarlett because of its potential value to our mission, but you've gone too far. You have forgotten who you are. I will stay here to continue with the mission I was given. Nothing more. Now, I believe we have a commitment to attend to," he concluded, referring to our dinner engagement with the Haringtons. He seemed determined to resume with the mission, using the opportunity to both observe and experience authentic human interaction.

"Petyr, you can't afford to waste time participating in another futile charade. We must leave soon to get to Empyrian before Aris makes a move. I can feel his impatience," Kara urged.

She was right. The best thing to do would be to leave now, but there was no way I could disappear from Scarlett's life without an explanation. "I'm going to have dinner with the Haringtons, and so are you."

Scarlett opened the door, barely glancing at Kara before she took my hand and pulled me closer to her. "You're here."

"I said I would be," I whispered.

"What's the deal with these two?" Scarlett asked, amused more than puzzled.

Kara and Dru were standing next to each other, with Dru's arm placed awkwardly on Kara's shoulders.

"You should be grateful I'm finally joining this little charade of yours," Kara responded, saving me from having to lie.

"You remember Kara, don't you? My beautiful girlfriend." Dru's tone was convincing enough, but Scarlett merely rolled her eyes.

"I'd be grateful if you could let us in." Nero spoke with an unfaultable politeness that any human would appreciate, but not Scarlett.

"Please," she said in an embellished formality that matched, yet subtly mocked, Nero's.

In the dining room, Jack was helping his father, Jon, set the placements. He carried a tray of cutlery, following his father around the oval mahogany table.

"Nero! You're finally here. I've been waiting! Do you have one?" Jack carelessly dropped the tray on the table and ran to Nero, eager to find out what kind of gemstone Nero had brought for him this time.

"Someone's impatient." Scarlett shook her head as she ruffled Jack's thick, blond hair.

"Now, what happened to my cutlery officer? He seemed to have abandoned his post. I guess half of us will just have to eat with our hands. What a shame," Jon said, shaking his head dramatically.

"I'll be right back dad, okay? I just need to see something important."

"Your duty calls, buddy." Nero knelt down to match Jack's eye level and continued before disappointment settled on the child's face. "I tell you what, go finish what you've started and I promise a rainbow in your hand."

"A rainbow?"

"Just like a real one." Nero winked.

"Is that a bribe I hear?" Scarlett's mother, Helen, asked through a grin.

"Just a well-deserved reward. Isn't that right Jack?"

"Uh-uh." Jack nodded with enthusiasm. He hurried back to the table and picked up the tray of cutlery.

I helped Helen bring the food from the kitchen whilst the rest made their way to the table. From our very first dinner at the Harington's, my place had been in the chair between Scarlett and Dru. A convenient position. Not only did I have the expediency of monitoring Dru's physical challenges, I was also able to reach for Scarlett's hand to avoid having a pile of torn up pieces of tissue paper on the table. Something she did whenever her parents talked about things that made her feel uncomfortable, particularly stories about her childhood. Helen, Jack, and Nero usually sat on the opposite side of the table. Jack didn't mind his mother's frequent inspection of his vegetable consumption. He was always too immersed in asking Nero questions regarding their mineral collection.

Jon's position, however, wasn't influenced by physical or logical necessity. He claimed the symbolic eminence of being the head of household. It was interesting to find the association of space with authority in this world. This was the first apparent parallel between humans and Empyrs. It had allowed me to indulge in the hope that *maybe* Scarlett and I were not so different after all, and *maybe* there was a future for us. But this hope didn't exist right now.

The only space left was on the other end of the table opposite Jon, which would have been the best place for Kara. Not only would she appreciate the symbolism that accompanied this particular place, but she would also appear to sit next to Dru without being too close. Even the slightest distance between the two would have made this task more tolerable. Especially to Dru, who wasn't the most proficient when it came to hiding his distress. However, as I returned to the dining room with a bowl of salad in hand, I wasn't surprised to see Kara occupying my usual place at the table. I expected that, due to her considerate nature, Helen would make sure the newcomer sat in the middle, where she wouldn't feel left out.

"I thought Kara would be more comfortable there. You don't mind, dear, do you?" Helen asked when she caught me glancing at my usual chair.

"It's not a problem," I lied.

I attempted to conceal my disillusion as I made my way to my newly designated chair. I didn't say much throughout dinner. Somehow, I no longer felt like I was a part of it. I was already an outsider, listening to every voice, trying harder to remember every tone. I clung to every shade of light in the room, every sound, every movement, every expression, and every sensation being swiftly taken from me by each fleeting moment.

I had time, however short. I had time to ignore Kara's persistent reminder of the crisis looming outside these comforting walls, to focus on remembering. Creating mental images of memories was usually an effortless, mechanical act. This time, I couldn't afford to miss any detail. I'd need to remember this in its entirety, from the physical aspects to the extraordinary warmth it brought within me. It would remind me that this was one of the many things I couldn't take away from Scarlett. I hoped it would give me the strength to stay away.

After dinner, I sat on the sofa next to Scarlett. Though still carefully committing every single moment in my memory, a part of me paid close attention to Nero. As he handed the Saffiria stone to Jack, it became clear he was willing to disclose a dangerous extent of our reality to the humans—in front of Kara.

I knew everything there was to know about the stone, including where and how Nero acquired it. Still, I listened to Nero's every word. He narrated the way he had soared high up into the sky, lifting himself above the space of Turmoil and Endless Night to get to Saffir—a space where all seasons existed within one harmonious flow.

Jack was just as engrossed in this story as he had been in every other origin of the other stones Nero had given him. There was an undeniable glimmer in Jack's eyes as Nero described the seasons that simultaneously existed on Saffir. He began with how the bright heat of the summer slowly diffused into a soft touch of crimson, just as the vibrant flowers gently shriveled back into the soil. The green leaves from the surrounding trees were unable to overcome the russet weakness, rendering each leaf unable to hold on to its branch.

Nero allowed Jack to access images meant only for an Astra, encouraging him to imagine himself standing at the center of the space surrounded by the stream of seasons, drifting and changing, flowing continuously from one color, mood, temperature, and composition to the next. All were connected, yet each was distinct. From the brilliance of the heat to the pallor of the frost. From the growth of a blossoming seed to the deterioration of a crumbling life.

Jack wasn't the only person in the room mesmerized by the images. Nero was aware he was also sharing them with Dru and Kara. Dru's expression was almost identical to Jack's candid astonishment. Kara's face was plastered with greed for information that wouldn't normally be accessible to her Corta. Nero would have known this greed was strong enough to delay her logic, long enough for him to keep his promise to Jack before Kara could stop him.

"If you know how to read it, it can tell you the mood of the weather. This evening, it's cold but not windy, so this part right here"—Nero pointed at the center of the stone—"is opaque and gray, but if you look here on the edges, can you see these dark blue ripples?" He held the stone closer to Jack.

"Uh-huh." Jack nodded without taking his eyes off the stone.

"It means there's rain rolling toward our direction. Watch as it moves ever so slowly. Can you see it fade as it gets closer?"

Jack stared at the stone for a few seconds. Again, he nodded in excitement. "Yes, I see it, there, that part is fading."

"That's right. It means it'll just be a little drizzle when it gets here in six hours and seventeen minutes." It was dangerously precise information to disclose, but the Haringtons would all be fast asleep before they could confirm its accuracy.

"How do you know exactly when the rain will get here?"

"That's where it gets a little more complicated. These lines here around the ripple, they tell you how fast the rain is moving, and these dots in between can help you measure the distance. You have to add up the lines and the dots then convert them to human time."

Kara winced at the phrase, *human time*.

If you don't do anything, I will, her hostile voice pierced through my head.

I turned my gaze to the humans, encouraging her to do the same. Kara didn't know enough about the humans to understand the reason behind Jon and Helen's apparent indifference to Nero's alarming confessions.

She tilted her head toward me, and her words blasted so loud in my mind I almost visibly flinched.

They already know about us! How could you—

Before she could continue to assault my mind with her severe inner voice, I discreetly shook my head without meeting her gaze. One of the most important things I learned about the humans was their unwillingness to consider anything that bore any potential disruption to the monotony of their accepted reality. Generations after generations yielded to defense mechanisms in the form of fairy tales, myths, legends, and fantasies to give excuses to anything their unassuming reality didn't provide an explanation for. This was one of the major reasons why not a single human had ever realized just how different we were from them. This was also the reason both Jon and Helen paid no attention to Nero's confessions. They simply smiled at their son's innocence, his gullibility.

Kara, too, saw Jack as an innocent being whose thoughts were irrelevant. In spite of the fact that Jack believed Nero, who had given him access to knowledge of different worlds not even Kara could reach, she still didn't see him as a threat.

Nero saw Jack differently though. He believed children were the most perceptive form of humans. They hadn't been fully exposed to the realities of their world. Their minds were more open to see and accept alternatives. Their innocent view of their own world was, for Nero, a bridge toward superior wisdom.

"I'll give you the conversions. I believe you can master it. What do you think?" Nero continued to address Jack, ignoring Kara's increasing aggravation.

"I don't think I'm good at making them work." Jack shrugged. For the first time since Nero showed him the Saffiria stone, there was no excitement in his voice. "I tried what you said about the one that copies feelings on Dad, but it didn't work."

Both Jon and Helen shot Nero a warning glance, perhaps to inform him that Jack was getting close to discovering the truth behind what they believed to be fantasy. Instead of mocking their naivety, Nero gave them a warm smile, an indication that he had everything under control, before responding to Jack's concerns. "That doesn't mean you can't get better. You just need to be a little more patient. It's a skill you need to develop, just like reading or tying your shoelaces. You need practice. I'm going to write down the conversions and instructions for each stone, so you can always go back to the ones you find difficult."

"I'll try to learn them all," Jack affirmed, though he was still hesitant.

"There's no rush," Nero encouraged him.

"Speaking of rush, we have to go." Kara spoke voluntarily for the first time since she entered the Harington's home.

"Are you leaving?" Jon's gaze automatically fell onto his watch. Apart from Jack, no one seemed to be impressed by an alien stone that could predict the weather. However, hearing that we were leaving slightly earlier than we usually did was enough to catch their attention—humans and their inherent need to protect their routines.

"You have to go?" Scarlett's question was brief, but I could tell there was so much more she wanted to ask. Like Kara, she hadn't said anything that wasn't a reply to a question or a direct comment toward her. Even then, her responses were reserved. She knew us well enough to realize something was wrong, but I didn't want to address it until I absolutely had to.

"We can stay for a little while longer." I answered Scarlett and Jon's questions, but my eyes were fixed on Kara's.

"You have somewhere to be," Kara insisted, her voice was calmer than I expected.

"Anything important?" Jon's question was directed at Kara. Though she hadn't been willing to be part of our charade, she proved to be cooperative tonight. She flashed a warm smile and answered Jon's question. "Petyr has to go to his"—she paused though not long enough to highlight her hesitation—"Parents' house tonight. He needs to leave in good time."

Dru must have known more about the human conventions than we gave him credit for. He interrupted before anyone noticed Kara's peculiar concern over the personal business of her supposed boyfriend's friend. "What would we do without you?" he said, pulling Kara slightly closer to him and continued without taking his eyes off her, "She's the most organized person you'll ever meet. I don't know how she does it, but she doesn't seem to forget a thing. We all take advantage asking her to remind us about everything." This was the closest they'd ever allowed themselves to be. Kara had removed her coat when she entered the house, leaving her with a short-sleeved top. It was fortunate Dru had the good sense of keeping his long-sleeved jumper and putting his gloves back on after dinner. The layer of fabric that separated the Arca and the Agua had certainly helped, but I could tell Kara still found the proximity barely tolerable. Dru, on the other hand, seemed to be more at ease.

Kara pulled away as soon as she could without breaking the pretense. "With such lovely company, I can see why it would be so easy for him to lose track of time."

Both Jon and Helen believed every word. They smiled and returned the compliment, but Scarlett knew better.

I could feel her looking at me, waiting for me to catch her eyes. I held her hand, hoping it would be enough to assure her she would get her explanation.

I thanked Kara for her thoughtfulness, but insisted I could afford to stay a little longer, then turned my attention back to Nero who had resumed his demonstration.

Kara sighed, but she didn't say anymore, not even in my head.

"I guess everyone gets to see that rainbow I promised." Nero winked at Jack whose jaw dropped the instant he heard the word *rainbow*.

"Why do you look so surprised? Did you think I wasn't going to keep my promise?"

"No, but . . ."

It was amusing to see Jack's uncertainty on how to articulate the doubts caused by the conflict between his desire to believe and the faint voice of his human logic. As though determined to remove the doubt from Jack's mind, Nero took the child's hand and placed the stone in the middle of his palm. "When you put the stone exactly there, you can think of any type of weather condition and the stone will show it. Now, think of a rainbow, and try to picture it clearly in your head."

Jack closed his eyes for a few seconds. When he opened them, a vibrant rainbow was oozing from the middle of the stone into his palm.

"That looks very impressive. The light reflection is spectacular. How many batteries does it take?" Jon asked in a low voice to ensure that Jack, who was still immersed in his rainbow, couldn't hear him.

"You haven't spent too much on this, have you?" Helen added, attempting to be equally discreet. As expected, both Jon and Helen refused to see what was right in front of them.

"Not even a penny. As I said, I picked it up from the cosmos, above the space of Turmoil and Endless Night," Nero replied.

Both Jon and Helen would have assumed the reason for Nero's answer was the possibility that Jack could hear, but I knew it was more than that. It was an uncharacteristically risky act for Nero to do. It seemed that he wanted to test and push the limits of the humans.

"Can I try something else?"

I leaned forward knowing Nero would say yes, and I had to stop him. "Maybe you should put it away now. It would be such a shame if it gets damaged before you can even learn to read it."

"I really want to see something else. Can I? Please, please?" Jack asked Nero, ignoring my suggestions.

"Of course you can. It's yours."

"Nero," I whispered, allowing him to see the doubts and concern in my expression.

"Go for it, Jack." He, too, ignored me.

I could have tried harder, but it was no longer my place. What right did I have to question Nero's judgment and intention when I was the one who betrayed our kind?

Within seconds, a translucent element appeared, swirling around the middle of the stone. I knew exactly what was coming. I had seen this many times before, but like everyone else in the room, my eyes were bound to the element. It gradually increased in speed, sweeping into wider, circular motions until the top covered the entire circumference of the stone. Within seconds, the translucent element emerged into a dark aggressive force, tamed only by its own strict motion.

Everyone was silent. Admiration drowned the questions as they beheld a tornado spinning in the palm of a child. Merely four inches in height, the tornado evoked the same hostility as that of one forty feet high. Everyone could sense the impact, but only Nero and I knew the extent of its reality.

"Can you feel the wind around your palm?" Nero asked Jack.

"I can," Jack whispered, moving his free hand to touch the tornado.

"You don't want to do that," I warned him, but as expected, he ignored me. Instead, he faced Nero, hoping for consent. When Nero shook his head, Jack pulled his hand away without question. Nero had clearly earned the boy's trust. Even if it meant giving Kara and Dru a reason to question his judgment.

Though I knew Nero was aware of the limits, I couldn't leave knowing the risk. "Amazing piece of technology, isn't it?" I asked Jon discreetly, ensuring not to catch Jack's attention.

There was a brief, thoughtful pause before Jon replied, "What will they think of next, eh?" The most predictable aspect of the humans was their inherent need for a familiar explanation. This, of course, was no longer true for Scarlett. After learning about my true nature, irrespective of how much she could understand of the limited information I revealed, she had been constantly aware.

"Pete, let's go to the garden so I can give you the plant I wanted you to take to your parents' house." She stood up at once without waiting for a reply.

I followed, knowing she was leading me toward the place where I'd have to break a promise.

"What's going on?" Scarlett asked when we reached the garden.

I took a deep breath, hoping the air would be kind enough to drown my voice, to stop me from letting the words out.

But the air felt harsh in my throat as Scarlett's eyes held mine, pleading for the truth.

"Why is Kara here? Where are you going?"

I attempted to form the words to answer her, but each syllable melted with the overwhelming heat that burned in my chest. The heat clawed its way to my throat, and I felt its cruel sting in the rims of my eyes. I could barely control my voice when I finally managed to say, "You're in danger."

Scarlett didn't seem to share the same fear that tormented my senses. "I know, you said. What's the plan? Do we need to leave?" From the composure and resilience that resounded in her voice, it was clear she trusted me enough to believe everything was going to be fine. She was right. I was going to do everything in my power to make sure she was safe.

"You have to know why you're in danger." One of the many things she deserved from me.

"I already do." She appeared calm. "We aren't supposed to be together, and that Leera, she came to tell you the Supreme Eltors know you're spending too much time with a human." She smiled lightly at her last words. "I don't care. We'll get through this. We'll show them what we have is a good thing. Just tell me what I have to do."

"You don't have to do anything. You just have to let me do what *I have* to."

"I'm not sure I like the sound of that." She hesitated for the first time.

"We can't convince them to approve of our relationship. There's one more thing you have to know about me. I'm a different kind of Astra."

"A different kind?"

Before I could answer, Nero stepped into the garden. He didn't say anything, but he allowed me to see his ambivalence. If I told Scarlett the entirety of my identity, Dru and Kara would also receive the confirmation. When I nodded to confirm I was certain this was what I had to do, he stepped back into the house.

"Yes, the kind that generations of Supreme Eltors spent thousands of years waiting for. The kind that most Empyrs still believe to be nothing more than a myth." I could feel the distance between us, now almost tangible, expanding, as I revealed more about my true nature.

"You must be something special." She tried to sound humorous, but the tears that glazed her eyes betrayed her.

"As you know Empyrs have harmony with certain elements depending on our Corta; Astra with wind, Arca with earth and Agua with water. I, on the other hand, have access to every element. If I choose to, I'm able to control them, including fire. I can make any world crumble with very little effort."

"Like a god."

"No, not like a god, just an immense cosmic danger. I'm what they refer to as the *Shield* of Empyrian. The identity of the *Shield* had always been a guarded secret, but the belief in the existence of the being with such power had been encouraged to ensure the other worlds would know better than to attempt anything destructive to Empyrian. You see, when I admitted to myself how much I loved you, it opened up possibilities and risks the Supreme Eltors are not willing to take."

"I get it. They can't afford to lose control of you, not with the power and the threat you possess," she said, continuing my thought. "What do you have to do now?" Her voice quivered as she asked the question she already knew the answer to.

"I have to leave." Tears flowed from Scarlett's eyes as I said the words we both dreaded to hear. I pulled her close to me and wrapped my arms around her. "I don't want to," I whispered, "but I have to."

"We can deal with this together." She struggled to speak.

I placed my hands on her shoulders and slightly pushed her back, willing her to see the truth in my expression. "This is the only way to ensure your safety." I needed her to hear it. I needed her to understand.

She didn't hold my gaze this time. Instead, she turned away as she said, "You promised you wouldn't leave. When you told me what you were, you promised you'd stay here, with me."

"You know I would if I could."

Her pleading eyes found mine again. "We'll find another way. We'll talk to them together. We'll run. We'll hide. I don't care. Just don't leave."

"When it comes to you, your life, I can't take the risk. I will suffer anything if it means you can stay alive."

Kara's voice echoed in my mind. *Petyr, we have to go. Now.*

I wanted to say so much more to Scarlett, but time was running out. There was only one thing I could say to help her let me go. "If I stay, you and everyone you love will die."

She was silent for a few seconds. I could see she wanted to say she didn't care, but she couldn't risk the lives of her family as much as I couldn't risk hers. I left her with no choice. She had to let me go. With that realization, she pulled me into her arms, held me for a few seconds, and walked away.

Every step confirmed the irrevocable distance between us. We had never truly been together; we were of different worlds, different timeframes. The most logical option was to accept our separate fates.

Kara and Dru approached me when Scarlett disappeared into the house.

"I'm sorry, Pete," Dru said as he stepped beside me, placing his gloved hand on my shoulder.

"Dru, what you said before—"

"Yes, I won't let any harm come to her," he affirmed before I could even finish asking. The tranquility and confidence in his voice willed me to have full confidence in his ability. Unlike me, Dru seemed to have learned and grown stronger in this world.

"We have to go." Kara spoke with the same sense of urgency that her inner voice carried.

I gave Kara a single nod, and almost at once, she drifted into the dark mist. I should have followed her immediately. I should have been rational enough to ignore the sound of light, clumsy footsteps treading toward me.

"I know what I'm risking, but I trust you. I heard what you said earlier, but I have to ask you again. Face this with me. Stay."

Scarlett trusted me. She expected me to do better, to have a better solution, to stop her pain, to save everyone without having to break her heart.

But I had nothing.

The scorching pain in my throat blazed again, rendering me incapable of speaking. I wanted to tell her something that would make her feel better, but I refused to lie to her. Though she didn't say another word, her wounded eyes pleaded loud enough that I almost allowed myself to pull her into my arms and take her with me. No. It wasn't an option. This time, I had to be rational. I wiped the tears from her cheeks and let my hand linger against her skin. For those few inimitable seconds, I could pretend I didn't have to let go.

It was all I had left with her: seconds. I let go, turned my back, and jumped.

I leapt higher with each jump, creating more distance from the ground that clung to my feet, but I gasped for the kind of air I'd never find in this world. I needed something to remind me of my old self. I needed to be rational, now more than ever. The Supreme Eltors must not see my despair. I needed to convince them that Scarlett hadn't corrupted me— the Empyr, the Astra, the Eltor, the *Shield* was back where he belonged. No further action would be necessary.

I could no longer ignore the distinct feeling I'd been trying to bury beneath all the emotions rushing through me.

It wasn't fear, but it held an ominous quality. This wasn't about the Supreme Eltors. I had to admit this was one of those rare moments when I needed to ask for Nero's opinion. Despite our differences, Nero had always been a vital part of my existence, one of the very few Empyrs who knew the full extent of my abilities. He had never let it stop him from helping my development as an Eltor. He'd always taken more responsibilities than he was given, and I was certain that even now, he blamed himself for my mistakes.

I feel it, too. Kara's voice echoed in my mind, interrupting my thoughts.

I looked over at Kara, waiting for an indication to stop and figure out the threat that was clearly closer than the one waiting for us in Empyrian. She stood still, yet she was advancing almost as fast as I was. She had a connection with water, but she didn't have the same relationship with it Dru had with nature or I had with the wind. Kara commanded water, drawing it from different sources around her—condensation on the leaves, damp residues in the soil, misty air, cloud—and controlling each droplet to unnaturally conform to her desires. She interfered with the flow of wind, forcing the sprays of fresh dew to expand and freeze into dull and heavy fragments. Kara's Corta saw everything as inferior, including the most vital element in their ability, in their survival. Water was nothing but a tool for the Agua, and in this case, the sharp pallets of barren hail were ordered to lift Kara off the ground and transport her.

On the surface, it seemed Kara had an effortless superiority. She could detect the slightest change in my sentiment, or even those who were in a different world, whilst taking stern control of the dense droplets of water around her. However, there was a distinct harshness in the element's movement. Though careful not to disrupt Kara's posture, the pellets that stirred around her often collided, leaving a trail of broken pieces of frozen water behind. I could tell Kara was struggling to stay in control, trying to do too much at once.

Don't worry about my ability. Focus on your own. You're the one who needs to convince them. Kara clearly noticed my unease. Her familiar firmness was back in the voice that resonated in my mind.

I spent the rest of the journey to Empyrian focused on burying Scarlett's face in the deepest part of my mind. Even though I was certain I had been changed forever, I needed to appear to be my old self again, just long enough to convince Supreme Eltors.

VIII. JOURNEY

You have more decisions to make, Kara warned me as we approached the passage.

"Decisions?" I turned when she landed behind me.

Instead of answering, she gave a single nod, gesturing for me to look ahead.

In the distance, a figure with careless posture leaned on the broad trunk of a leafless tree. A smile, more polished than usual, broke from his face.

"Dru, what are you doing here?"

Before he could answer, another figure stepped out of the shadows.

"Are you not happy to see us?" Nero asked with unusual warmth in his voice.

I knew I wasn't jumping as fast as I usually did. I was in no rush to leave this world, but I still found it surprising they got here before us. My Exir must be much weaker than I hoped. I was grateful to see them both, but the only possible reason for them to be here was to tell me they had decided to join me back to Empyrian. That wouldn't be logical. Nero wouldn't abandon his responsibilities and Dru had to stay to help ensure everyone's safety, particularly Scarlett's.

"We have a plan." He smiled through his words.

I knew what he meant, but I hoped I was wrong.

I was not.

Scarlett appeared from behind the tree Dru was leaning on.

The very moment my eyes found hers, I was drawn to her. There was no mental process, just instinct. I held her in my arms. The burning hole in my chest that I'd been fighting so hard to cover up faded. I felt whole again.

"What are you doing here?" I forced myself to speak, the words barely audible.

"I'm going with you." She placed her hands on my face and pulled me into a kiss that demanded my surrender.

"I can't." These words were even harder to speak than I could have imagined. I wasn't sure if she heard me. A part of me hoped she didn't. I couldn't hurt her again. I couldn't turn my back on her again.

This wasn't fair. She shouldn't be here.

"Why did you bring her here?" I addressed Dru more harshly than I ever had before.

"It seemed like a good idea," Dru replied, his expression laced with such certainty, such confidence.

"Good idea? So you can all see me turn my back on her again?"

Dru didn't respond. My manner should offend him, but there was no resentment in his calm expression. I knew he wasn't to blame. This wouldn't have been his idea. Still, he promised to protect her, yet he allowed her to come here, where I could wound her. Again.

"Petyr, it's not Dru's fault," Nero said. "I didn't want to get involved earlier. I wasn't willing to contradict the Supreme Eltors overtly. I also thought you'd realize the option—"

"I know the option," I interrupted, "but it's not one I'm willing to pursue. I won't place her in more risk than she already is." I couldn't possibly let her join me back to Empyrian. It was too dangerous. The whole reason behind my journey was to convince the Supreme Eltors not to come to this world, to keep them away from Scarlett.

My world would also be far too different from everything her senses had been conditioned to. From the spectrum of colors, to the sounds, the structures, the air . . . I couldn't be sure if Scarlett's mind and body would be able to handle such change.

"She knows the risks. We have explained everything to her." Nero remained calm.

"That doesn't change—"

"I can see you care about Scarlett too much to take even the most calculated risk, but she can handle it, Petyr. Her mind will shut down, but it will recover and adapt to the new environment. Evan can help you make sure of that."

Though he kept his composure, I could hear the impatience in Nero's voice. He always found pleasure in providing information, in being the one who knew the answers, but he wasn't used to having to give the answers to an Astra.

"It's easy to calculate those odds, but we can't be sure," I continued my protest. "There is no proof. No human has ever set foot in Empyrian."

"I know. But I'm a very skilled Astra." He sighed. I could tell he was finding it difficult to believe he had to remind me of the extent of our capabilities. "And so are you, which is why you know I'm not wrong."

"How about the Supreme Eltors?" I didn't voice my question to undermine his notions. I knew he would have an answer, and I needed to hear his reassurance.

"This, you should have figured out yourself." Nero's voice was stern. His eyes pierced me, almost commanding me back to my senses. "You can't let the way you feel about Scarlett blind you from all logic. You can't afford to keep making the wrong decisions. If you were to stand any chance at convincing them, you can't keep missing the obvious. The Supreme Eltors, Petyr, won't expect her to be there, which makes Empyrian the safest place for her."

Nero was right. I needed to regain my confidence and be the sharp, rational Astra I was. But I needed his reassurance, one last time. My voice was tentative as I asked, "And Aris?"

"There will be a chance, when you get there, for Aris to detect her presence," Nero admitted.

"You say that like it is nothing to worry about." I protested, but in truth, I was hopeful Nero would give me a rational explanation.

He ignored my remark and continued, "Aris, like the Supreme Eltors, won't expect her to be there, and therefore he won't be monitoring her. Once you reach Evan, she won't be detected."

"Unless Evan lets them know. We'll be placing our fates in the hands of a Spark. Does that sound logical to you, Nero?" This time, my disapproval was genuine.

"What's wrong with that? Can't we trust Sparks? Aren't they Empyrs, too?" Scarlett asked.

Kara answered first. "No, they're not worthy of being called Empyrs. They're weak and—"

Nero interjected, "Creating an Empyr is a critical process. When we transform into our Exir, we're bound to seek an equal from the same Corta. Both Exirs have to be at their strongest, compatible in every respect. Strengthening the Exir so it's prepared to reproduce takes more than four centuries. Finding one's absolute compatible could take even longer. Each Empyr must be created from perfection. However, there are those either less calculated or too impatient to accept their Exirs aren't ready. Thus, producing a Spark."

"Right, so Sparks are flawed. In what way? Are they naturally evil or just not as strong and smart as you? Because if it's the latter, then I think we're overreacting." Scarlett asserted, trying to add a shade of humor in her statement, but I could see how serious she was in attempting to figure out if Evan could be trusted.

"Sparks have a very weak Exir, too weak to flourish," I said. "They aren't able to transform, so they're trapped in their Nherum form their entire existence. Their lives end with their physical form. They have no Corta. They have no real purpose, no allegiance to anything. That's why we can't trust them."

"Your kind sure has little tolerance for weakness." She'd lost the humor in her tone. "You're meant to be flawless, and a Spark is a reminder that weakness has its consequences. How ironic that you need a Spark's help to save a human."

I winced at the real irony of seeking the help of a Spark to remedy the consequence of an Eltor's weakness.

"Trusting Evan is our best option."

I found it difficult to ignore the seamless blend of sincerity and certainty in Nero's response.

"We have to trust him then," Scarlett agreed with Nero, then turned to me. She took my hand in hers and asked, "Why are you trying so hard to find excuses to be away from me?"

"I'm trying to keep you safe." I didn't know how else I could say those words to make her understand. There was nothing I wanted more than to have her with me, but I couldn't do it knowing her life would be at risk. I couldn't be selfish, not this time.

"You heard Nero. Empyrian is the safest place for me. And if I'm there, there's no reason for them to come here. That means my family is safer too."

Somehow, Scarlett's voice anchored my frenzied mind. She, too, wanted me to hear her earnest words.

"They're right, Pete." Dru's voice was composed, further emphasizing I was the only one falling apart. "Evan may be a Spark, but we all know he's very skilled. He can keep Scarlett safe even if the Supreme Eltors realize she's there. Plus, he'd never help the Supreme Eltors. I mean, he's a Spark."

"The plan makes sense," Kara said firmly. "I will try to keep Aris focused on Petyr." She didn't try to impose superiority by either dominating or sabotaging the group's plan. She didn't mock Dru's intellect or insult Scarlett's presence. I found myself conflicted with doubt for Kara's motives but grateful for her graciousness.

Everyone had spoken, and they'd all considered Scarlett's safety. I'd have to trust them more than I trusted my own— unreliable—senses. Scarlett would go to Empyrian, and I'd do *everything* to keep her safe.

"Fine," I finally said then turned to Dru. "I apologize for my discourtesy. I know you're only trying to help."

"I understand." Dru smiled, but as soon as his gloved hand touched my shoulder, I saw a strain in his eyes. He turned away before his smile could dissolve. I didn't have to see his face to recognize the pity he felt for me.

"I guess it's time for me to go," Nero announced.

"You're not coming?" I didn't try to hide the disappointment in my voice.

"Someone has to be here to continue with the mission." I could detect the ambivalence in Nero's voice. He wanted to help us, but he chose not to turn his back on Scarlett's family. He gave me a single nod, and with solemn certainty said, "I will see you all soon." Then, he jumped.

"What do we do now?" Scarlett asked after Nero had gone.

"Now we take a leap, and we fall to Empyrian," Dru answered.

"Fall?" Scarlett followed Dru's gaze. She took a couple of deep breaths and hesitantly stepped to the edge of the cliff. Leaning over the edge, she seemed to confirm what she had been dreading. She failed to contain a loud gasp as her stunned eyes wandered down the precipice. The steep, sheer face of a rocky slope dropped down for miles. "Are we really going to jump off this cliff?"

"It's not what it seems," I reassured her.

"I was hoping you'd say that." She tried to smile, but she couldn't cover her apprehension. "So what happens when we jump?"

"We don't know," Dru answered before I could.

"You don't know?" she asked slowly, perhaps hoping she misheard.

"Well, this isn't the way we came." Dru shrugged.

The anxiety in Scarlett's eyes was more evident now, so I offered immediate reassurance. "I do know that it's safe and that it'll only take a few minutes and—"

"We've wasted enough time," Kara interrupted. "Just let her see for herself." She walked toward the very edge of the cliff, beside Scarlett, who reflexively stepped a couple of paces back. Kara turned around to face me, spread her arms, and said, "Don't take too long." She let herself fall backward into the wild breeze.

"My turn," Dru said. He took a few steps back and ran toward the edge. "See you on the other side!" he screamed as he launched himself into the air. He plunged down with his knees bent up to his chest, arms wrapped around his folded legs.

"I guess it's our turn now," Scarlett said with less than her usual confidence.

"Don't worry. I'll be right here. I won't let go of you," I promised.

"I know." She forced a tentative smile. "I'm still anxious though. It's human nature," she added in a lighthearted tone.

"Are you ready?" I whispered.

She took a deep breath before she answered, "As I'll ever be."

She wrapped her arms around my neck the way she did whenever she jumped with me. I placed my hands on her waist, lifted her up, and carried her to the edge of the cliff. As I leaned forward to push us gently toward the empty space behind her, I moved my right hand to the back of her neck and my left to her lower back for support. Then, we jumped.

I could feel immediate panic overcoming Scarlett. I held her closer, trying to calm her body that shuddered beneath mine. I held her head in place so her face was directly in front of mine. "It's okay. It's okay. I'm here. Just look at me." I repeated my words until her glistened eyes found mine, and finally, I felt her gradual calmness.

"Don't let me go."

Her request was painfully familiar. I realized now why she was so afraid. She no longer had the same trust in me. She'd never admit it, or even acknowledge it, but I knew I'd lost a part of her. She would always know I was capable of deserting her. I wanted to be better for her, to make the right decisions. I hoped there was more I could do to make sure she felt safe in my arms again.

Her face was less than an inch away from mine, and her eyes were no less riveting than they had been all those times they rendered me incapable of speech. I was certain about how I felt. "I love you, Scarlett. I love you more than I can ever say."

She closed her eyes for a few seconds and held me tighter. "I know," she finally whispered. Her lips found mine, and she kissed me with more yearning than she ever had. I was lost in a few moments of intensity, suddenly aware of her warm body underneath mine.

Her hands slid from my neck down to my back until they found their way beneath my shirt. Her fingers and palms burned on my skin, sparking a deeper sense of desire within me. I kissed her, allowing myself to be led by desire, but all the while knowing I wasn't in danger of the *Forbidden*. I wanted to be close to Scarlett. Nothing more. I loved her. So I kissed her, with freedom.

The harsh pull of our fall stopped, leaving only the calm wind, gliding around us. We're in the final part of the passage—the *Haze*.

"Is it over?" Scarlett asked.

"No. It won't be long, but please, close your eyes."

"Why?"

"We're entering the *Haze*. You can't look—"

"What happens if I do?"

"I've never experienced it myself. They say you'll see and feel that which you fear the most, but if your mind is secure, then all you'd see is a thick white haze."

"What makes you think I'll see something? I want to try it."

The human mind was inherently disorganized. Their thoughts were scattered, erratic, and therefore I was certain Scarlett would see something. Before I could explain, she coughed out a bitter whimper. The force of her fingers dug into my skin. Her breathing grew heavy and urgent, like she was trying to scream but she hadn't the strength.

"I'm here," I said. "Nothing will hurt you. I'm here." I brushed the tears off her burning cheeks, and the lines of distress on her face smoothed. Somehow my words were enough to wane the assault of dread on her trembling body. She seemed to find the same serenity in my voice that I found in hers.

I turned us over so her body rested on mine. She remained still, her head on my chest. "Will I forget about it once we get out of here?"

"As far as I know, you won't forget, but you won't feel the fear with the same level of intensity." I knew it wasn't the answer she was hoping for, but it was the only one I had. Waiting for the next couple of minutes to pass was agonizing for Scarlett. I could tell she tried very hard to hide her fear and stop herself from trembling. I could hear the brisk, irregular sound of her heartbeat, and the rapid torrent of blood through her veins. Scarlett was still very afraid. The girl showed no fear when she stared in the eyes of the *Forbidden*, or when she touched my Exir. What could she have seen that made her so afraid?

I held my breath, and I looked into the *Haze* to face my own fear.

A boy.

His green eyes glistened with terror, anger, desperation . . . In the midst of all the ambivalence, he was hopeless.

He was desolate. Lost.

I felt everything.

IX. SPARK

It was familiar. The amethyst sky diffused with crimson radiance, emanating from the Astras that lived above, was an image I'd yearned for as I endured the suffocating barren sky in the human world.

The wind moved with the same gracefulness, coruscating in its divine translucence. It reflected the effulgent Empyrian light and embraced me with the same warmth it always had. Yet, the gem-encrusted ground gleamed coldly beneath my feet. The conviction to the idea of once again being able to leap above the Empyrian sky and reach the place where—I thought—I belonged, now felt like the desires of someone else.

For so long, I yearned for the space that would unbind me from any restrictions to act according to my nature. The kind of space only Empyrian could offer. But it now seemed unnecessary.

This was Empyrian. It was familiar, but it was no longer home.

"When you're ready, you can open your eyes slowly," I told Scarlett. "You'll feel discomfort, maybe pain, but not for long. Then, you'll lose consciousness. It's because—"

"I know, Nero explained everything to me. I'm ready," she interrupted, her weak voice willing me to believe she wasn't afraid.

"I'm sorry to put you through this—"

"Stop. You're not putting me through anything. This is my decision. I chose to be here. I'm pretty tough. You should know that by now." She managed to end with a hint of her usual spirited nature, reminding me of how much stronger she was than me.

"You're incredible," I whispered.

"I know." She smiled as she opened her eyes, but the smile soon faded into a wince as she confronted the Empyrian light.

"What can you see?" Dru voiced the question I wanted to ask.

"Bright," Scarlett responded after a few seconds, "and everything is fuzzy, like I'm underwater." She twitched, flinging her hands over her ears, as if attempting to stabilize a sharp pain.

I held her as she lost consciousness.

"We better move," said Dru. Though I kept my attention on Scarlett, I didn't miss the anxiety in his voice. "What's wrong?" I asked without taking my eyes off of Scarlett.

"Do you really need to ask? We're out in the open where they can very easily feel our presence." His voice was filled with more than just anxiety. There was a sense of aggression I hadn't heard from Dru before. Perhaps it was finally sinking in. He was risking too much to fight a battle that wasn't his.

"How was your fall?"

Dru didn't answer my question, but traces of unease still lingered in his expression.

Let's go. An unusual apprehension laced Kara's voice as it reached my mind. I could tell she, too, saw something. Neither of them would admit to it, just as I'd never let anyone know what I saw and felt in the *Haze.* Even the weakest of Empyrs would like to believe they could go through the *Haze* without seeing anything. We're Eltors. We're supposed to be fearless and flawless. But we're all afraid. *At least, I wasn't the only one,* I thought. The realization gave me a veil of comfort—however thin.

Without another word, Kara conjured her misty elements and glided forward.

Avoiding my gaze, Dru broke into a sprint to follow Kara, but he was much slower than usual. Whatever he saw in the *Haze* must have affected him greatly. I couldn't worry about Dru right now, not while I had Scarlett unconscious in my arms. We had to get a remedy, fast.

Even though I wasn't looking forward to reaching the Sparks' region, I jumped with urgency. Since Sparks had a detached culture from the rest of Empyrian, it wasn't a familiar place.

The Sparks' region, the Black Caves, was located on the edge of Empyrian. To get there, we had to pass the Great Evrass, the dwelling of the Arca. Only Dru would have the right to step in this part of Empyrian. Kara and I would have to tread the outskirts to get to the Black Caves. I prepared to pick up my speed, knowing Dru would be much faster inside his territory, surrounded by all the right elements.

But Dru stopped running.

He stood at the opening of the Great Evrass, staring into his home. All Kara and I could see were immense ancient trees with unnatural symmetry both in height and width, uniformly aligned, sternly fencing the Arcan space. Light dispersed with impeccable precision, allowing certain amount of darkness to exude a bleak, uninviting atmosphere. At the same time, leaving just enough vibrancy to highlight the most ideal shades of the green leaves, faded in all the right places to denote the life and rich beauty nature hid behind the dark exterior.

Dru moved one leg to step forward, but hesitated. Instead, he stretched one hand toward the tree in front of him. He spread his palm, like he was going to press it against the trunk, but stopped just a few inches before touching it. He closed his eyes and kept his hand there for a few seconds, perhaps trying to feel a connection with his element. He let out a bleak sigh, put his hand down, and opened his eyes.

Dru had spent most of his time in the human world yearning to be back to the one place where he knew he would be liberated from all the restrictions he suffered. Now, there he was, nothing more than a step away from his home, yet still restricted.

He stepped back, hesitant for a few seconds, and then sprinted along the outskirts of the Great Evrass. He moved with great speed, yet he was nowhere near as fast as he would have been if he were inside his terrain.

Kara pushed forward with an impatient sneer after muttering the words, *thoughtless* and *waste of time*.

There was peculiar tension in Dru's arms as he strived to keep up his speed. Despite Dru's unrefined manner when he ran, especially around nature, he always had such effortless precision. He could move in any direction, freely and swiftly, without disturbing a single life around him. But this time, he was too careful, too conscious. He was trying too hard to run faster, perhaps determined to distance himself from his home.

I glanced at Scarlett, still unconscious in my arms. I'd taken her from her home and I was doing the same to Dru. I could tell Dru was afraid to be close to his home because he didn't want to be distracted from the task at hand. But this wasn't his obligation. This was my trouble, caused by my weakness. How could I still have the woman I loved in my arms and my friends by my side? I had nothing to offer them.

If I faced the Supreme Eltors by myself, I'd appear stronger. But I did want my friends and Scarlett with me, irrationally and selfishly so. *They had made their own decision to be here, and I must respect it,* I thought, convincing myself to believe my own lie. I used this lie to suppress the guilt that came with the truth.

When we reached the end of the Great Evrass, the sky had faded into a distinct dullness. The air was heavier, the wind more abrupt. The Great Evrass was vast, but the distance we had yet to travel toward the Spark's region was even larger. We kept moving until the Great Evrass was no longer visible behind us.

I could see Kara was struggling to control the unruly mist that became more and more defiant the closer we got to the Black Caves. I felt less secure jumping on this part of Empyrian than I had the first time I jumped in the human world. Dru, on the other hand, seemed more at ease running along thousands of miles of desiccated land than when he was near his home. When we reached the Sparks' region, I could see both Kara and Dru felt the same sense of relief and dread I did.

We were silent for a few moments as we stood on the darker part of Empyrian. The vibrant amethyst sky had faded into a dark-gray veil, enclosing the recklessly brisk wind and the harsh, grating sound of the sea as the waves thrashed against the ancient scabrous rocks. The caves were scattered across a precipitous slope, leading down to the ocean.

"Which one is Evan's?" Dru asked.

Most Empyrs had never been on this part of Empyrian. There were three reasons for this. Empyrs naturally stayed in their own regions and respected the privacy of others. Most wouldn't want to be associated with Sparks. Finally, this region was far too unpredictable to warrant the tolerance of most Empyrs. The closer we got to it, the heavier the air felt, and the harder it was to control our physical abilities. The Sparks made sure those with a functioning Exir wouldn't be able to impose their superiority on them, at least not on their territory.

In succession, the caves disappeared, leaving only the one embedded onto the highest point of the precipice.

"We have to get going," I urged, attempting to conceal my surprise. I traced a little over six hundred meters along the coarse face of the cliff we would have to scale. I knew better than to jump. The heaviness in the air weighed vehemently on my shoulders, keeping me grounded.

Kara tried to will water particles to help boost her up, but soon resigned herself to the fact that in this part of the world, the elements didn't succumb to force. Despite my own frustration at the wind that burnt on my skin with each cruel blow, a part of me couldn't help but feel satisfaction with the sight of a helpless Agua. For the first time, Kara appeared unable to force unwilling elements and treat nature with such disrespect.

"Will you be fine going up with Scarlett?" Dru asked before we began our climb. It would make sense for him to be the one to carry Scarlett up the canyon. Not only was he stronger, but his skills were also augmented by physical contact with rocks and soil. Though I had no doubt he wouldn't find the abrasive rocky gradient as challenging as I would, I couldn't let someone else take the responsibility of ensuring Scarlett's safety. I needed to keep her close.

"I'll be fine." I wrapped one arm around Scarlett's waist, spreading my hand to support her back as her head leaned securely on my shoulder. With my other hand, I carefully traced the rough, uneven formation of the rocks. I grasped on to precise points before lifting both our bodies up, only a few inches at a time. Our slow ascent took a great deal of concentration and muscle coordination. Scaling the rocks without the support of the elements made it far more strenuous than I'd expected. I was so used to having the wind by my side that I never considered just how much I relied on it to enhance my skills. The strength and ability of my Nherum form remained, but without the provision of the wind, I wasn't completely confident. Especially not with Scarlett in my arms.

I tried not to get distracted by the fact that with every inch above the ground, I was risking Scarlett's life a little more. If I were to make a mistake and slip, I was unsure how willing the wind would be to assist our fall. Putting Scarlett in danger seemed to be the only consistent thing I had done since I met her. I'd broken many promises, but with this, I never failed to deliver.

Dru didn't climb as fast as I knew he could have. The apprehensive glances were confirmation he had been pacing himself for a reason. Every glance was motivated by worry and mistrust. I knew that glance well. It was the same one I'd given him as I monitored him while he ran in the human world.

The positions had been altered, and I was now the one who needed to be watched. It wasn't only the feeling of inferiority that made me uneasy, but also the subtle changes in Dru's temperament. He'd grown distant, careful. I knew he regretted his decision, but he manipulated his expressions to keep certain thoughts private. He concealed his hesitation to save me from guilt. As if guilt hadn't been a constant force polluting my sentiments. I could stop and speak to him, but I didn't want to hear the truth. *If he didn't want to be here, he would tell me*, I thought. It was easier to convince myself that the right thing to do was to let him carry on by my side. After all, I was far too occupied by the immense effort it took to control my already-chaotic mind, as well as fostering enough concentration to climb in the absence of the wind's support.

When we finally reached the top and stood in the shadow of the cave, I felt no sense of relief. Just more dread for the many possible challenges a bitter Spark had to offer. The cave's exterior was crude and menacing. Unrefined rocks suspended around a dark opening, exuding a sense of peril that was, no doubt, meant to make us feel uneasy.

Without a single word, Dru took a step forward and disappeared into the shadows. Kara's face was hard and vacant, evidently concealing the same sense of dread I tried to ignore. When she found my gaze, I nodded, and we stepped in at the same time. Once inside, the ground below our feet disintegrated into dust and we were falling. We were being sucked into a dark hole. The longer we fell, the more pugnacious the air pressure became.

We were inside a Spark's home, and I knew my senses were no longer my own. I yielded to what's left of my rationality and told myself that the rapid force pulling us down was nothing more than an illusion. Still, I held Scarlett tighter, ensuring she wouldn't slip through my arms. When the falling sensation stopped, the darkness faded into the interior of the cave, and the rock formations and stalagmites emerged.

"This seems to be the only way in."

I heard Dru's voice. I turned to find him standing next to me, pointing at the bottom of the wall a couple of meters ahead.

"No point trying to eliminate it to see how thick it is or what's behind. It doesn't work," he added when he noticed my eyes were focused on the wall in front of us. He was right. Apart from the narrow vertical space between the wall and the ground, there was no other possible way. Though we couldn't be certain how long we would have to crawl or what was waiting on the other side, it was clear this was what Evan wanted us to do to get to him.

"Are you sure you want to take Scarlett with you? I could stay here with her. Maybe, she'll be safer," Dru suggested.

"I will take her." No way would I leave Scarlett behind, and Dru knew better than to argue. He shrugged and walked toward the wall. Once again, he disappeared into the dark space without another word. Kara stayed behind to help me get Scarlett securely on my back.

With my body flat against the rough surface of the ground, I dragged us forward, ensuring Scarlett's back didn't scrape the wall that was a mere inch above her.

"If I ever see three Eltors crawling through a filthy cave to see a lowly Spark, well then, I'll be damned." Evan's condescendingly cheerful voice resounded.

The wall above us ascended until it disappeared into a dome-shaped ceiling, leaving us exposed, lying on the ground.

Something in Dru's expression told me he found the humor in this. Kara, on the other hand, was filled with fury as her thoughts echoed in my mind. She tried her best to pull herself up with grace before lending me a hand.

Obnoxious, filthy, worthless mistake of an existence!

Kara seemed to have pushed her voice into Dru's mind as well. Evan didn't miss the sudden discomfort in his expression.

"You scaled a mountain, plummeted into a dark pit, and crawled through dirt and mud to see me," he addressed Kara directly, with apparent tone of mockery. "Forgive me, Your Highness, but at this point, don't you think I deserve to at least hear your voice?" The grin on Evan's face was enough to show that his concern wasn't to hear her voice. It was to point out how he made an Agua bend to his will.

Kara wasn't admitting defeat. Her face didn't soften. She didn't utter a word. She didn't need to. She simply stared at Evan—menacingly, inducing regal authority.

For a second, Evan hesitated, but he managed to let out a short, casual laugh. "I'll take that as a no then."

Evan was in one corner of the empty cave, sat on a white plastic swivel chair with a chrome wheeled base. The chair was certainly out of place, not just in a cave. Plastic wasn't a typical material used in Empyrian. However, we were in a Spark's space, which meant appearances were not to be trusted. Over the centuries, they had spent too much effort trying to conceal the reality of their world, not that anyone was interested in knowing.

I heard Kara's voice in my mind. *I'm not the one who needs his help. I don't owe the worthless Spark anything.*

As though he heard Kara's thoughts, Evan replied, "Of course, you aren't the one who needs my help. You're just here for moral support, right?" He shook his head, letting out another condescending laugh.

Dru couldn't conceal a snicker. He seemed to appreciate the humor in Evan's determination to undercut Kara, something Dru himself had attempted to do many times before. This wasn't the only thing Dru and Evan had in common. They both had a carefree disposition. Youthful sense blazed in their wild, dark eyes that peeked through twisted locks of tousled, black hair. But Evan's eyes were much darker, with more depth, perhaps from experience, perhaps from pain.

"It's the Astra that needs help," Evan continued, turning his attention on me. "Imagine that, the one who has all the answers, the one who is always in control loses his supposedly all-knowing mind because of a human. What did she do? How enticing was the sound of her heartbeat?"

"That's enough," Dru demanded.

"Is it?" He addressed Dru without taking his eyes off me. "But I haven't even gotten to the interesting part." He let out a dry laugh to himself, but this time Dru didn't share his humor. "Do you have any idea what this one can do? He can click his fingers, and in an instant everything we know can implode."

"They know what I am." I regretted the sound of pride in my statement. Being the *Shield* was the one secret the others shouldn't have known.

"I know what they know, but I think they need to be reminded that every decision you make can affect the whole of Empyrian. That includes me and my people, so if there's a chance you'd choose to do something, let's say unnatural, then I say it's only fair that your Supreme Eltors are intending to do everything they can to stop you."

"Since you seem to know why we're here, it's time you gave us an answer. Can you help us?" I wasn't sure how he learned so much about me, or how much more he knew. I wasn't prepared to find out any more in front of Dru and Kara.

I was still allowing them to believe the lie that the Supreme Eltors were unjustified in their reaction to nothing more than a harmless thought. Knowing what they were risking for my sake, I couldn't stand here and admit that the night I confessed my identity to Scarlett was also the night I had willingly committed myself to turn my back on Empyrian—to turn my back on them. If they knew the extent of my betrayal, if they knew that the Supreme Eltors were only doing what was necessary, would they still be on my side? I wasn't prepared to learn the answer.

"I can help you. You knew that. That's why you're here. But will I? Well, that depends . . ."

"On what?" I asked, knowing he wouldn't continue until I did.

"On whether or not she is as special as you make her out to be." He nodded toward Scarlett, who remained unconscious in my arms. "I guess it's time to wake her up," he said as he lifted himself off the chair in one swift motion.

He tapped on the wall next to him. Then, layers of cream walls came down, unfolding piece by piece to cover the rough surface of the cave. The top part had also ascended into a cathedral ceiling with a skylight, showing a clear blue sky as opposed to the miserable gray reality outside. From the floor, now layered with carpet, ascended two oversized green sofas, two matching chairs, a round wooden coffee table, bookshelves, paintings, and various ornaments including urns, wooden sculptures and crystals. An almost exact replication of Scarlett's living room.

"We wouldn't want her to wake up in a cave now, would we? This ought to make her feel at home, don't you think?"

I could tell Evan was proud of what he had created and that he expected us to be impressed. I could also see that the other two were as suspicious as I was about how he knew what Scarlett's living room looked like.

"Place her over there," Evan ordered, pointing at the sofa. He was more assertive this time.

He managed to create the correct fabric texture and shape, but this sofa was triple the size of the one in Scarlett's living room. Evan managed to get the general image right, but there were many errors with certain details of the other furniture. Either his memory was far too unreliable, or he hadn't seen the place himself. He must have gotten the information from somewhere—or someone—else.

Evan's eyes lingered on my hand that held Scarlett's. He moved in front of me and kneeled on the floor. "Let's see," he mumbled to himself as he moved Scarlett's hair from her face. "I understand why you can't get her face off your mind. She's quite mesmerizing." His gaze remained fixed on Scarlett as he spoke.

Evan knew exactly how to get under one's skin, and he clearly reveled on anticipating the impact of his words. I did resent him for knowing as much as he did about my private concerns, about the nature of my relationship with Scarlett. I resented myself even more for causing a situation where I had to allow a Spark to impose a sense of authority over me. But I refused to give him the satisfaction of seeing me crumble. Damaged as I was, I was still an Astra, and concealing certain emotions and reaction from a Spark was something I was sure I could still manage. I focused on why we were here. He was helping Scarlett, and that's what mattered.

Evan extended his arm, palm open, like he was reaching to shake someone's hand. Almost in the same instant, a small, empty vial fell from the ceiling. His hand closed into a fist, clasping the bottle he caught without taking his eyes off Scarlett's face. In the same swift second, he flicked the cork off the bottle, placed his thumb on the opening, and moved his hand closer to Scarlett's face. When he removed his thumb from the opening, thick white vapor came gushing through, into Scarlett's nostrils. After a few seconds, he moved the bottle to Scarlett's ears. He did the same to her eyes, using his free hand to lift her eyelids. Having to watch him freely touch Scarlett made it increasingly difficult for me to conceal the signs of my unease. When the vapor finally ran out, Evan threw the bottle up into the air. It vanished before it could plummet back down.

Within seconds, Scarlett began to stir. I got up so I could step closer to her, but Evan raised his hand, gesturing for me to stop moving. There was a hyperbolic expression of uncertainty in his face. Of course, he was pretending, and he knew I'd realize this, but somehow, he also knew I'd still be worried. He faced me to confirm the evidence of anxiety in my expression. He shook his head and let out a victorious laugh.

I'd lost. A Spark had, with little effort, managed to trick an Astra into revealing his true emotions. He knew what I'd been hiding. He knew my weakness, and I was certain he knew so much more.

Scarlett opened her eyes, and none of it mattered. At least, in that moment, I didn't care about Evan and his motives. All I needed to know was that Scarlett was well.

"Good morning, beautiful." Evan breathed each word in soft tones and moved his face even closer to hers.

"Who-Who are you? Where . . . Petyr?" Scarlett managed to ask in her disorientated state.

"I'm here." I squeezed Scarlett's hand and nudged Evan out of the way.

"Hey." She smiled. She seemed to know I needed one.

"Hey." I had to stare for a few seconds as I relished the sense of relief. "How do you feel?"

"Okay, I guess." She looked around at the familiar surroundings and muttered, "Are we in—"

"No," I interrupted before disappointment could replace the warmth of her smile. "This is not your house."

"We're supposed to be in Empyrian," she stated, pushing herself up.

"We are." I didn't want to acknowledge the Sparks' region as part of Empyrian, but the division within our realm wasn't relevant information at the moment.

Evan's laughter caught Scarlett's attention, "You don't have to be polite on my account." He snickered and addressed

Scarlett. "Technically, you're in Empyrian, but the part he'd rather you didn't see. Well, the part he'd rather not see."

"We're in the Sparks' region," I clarified as Evan's words seemed to have added to her confusion.

"You're a Spark!" Scarlett exclaimed.

"Well, yes I am. What's so surprising?"

"I expected something"—perhaps realizing the implication of her statement, she tried and failed to find a better way to complete her sentence— "else."

But Evan simply shrugged and smiled, except this smile wasn't his usual dark and condescending one. I could tell this smile was meant to comfort Scarlett. "Lover boy didn't paint a good picture, huh. Don't worry. Not your fault."

"You made this place look like my living room," she said, changing the subject. "How did you know?"

"We'll have plenty of time for trivia later." Evan winked then turned his attention on me. "I see your problem here. She's interesting. She can stay. There's your answer. You have my help."

"What is he talking about?" Scarlett asked, but the weight in her voice told me that she already figured out my plan.

"Scarlett, you'll have to stay with Evan while I speak to the Supreme Eltors. I can't risk them finding you. This is the safest place for you," I urged.

"How about you? How do I know you'll be safe? Let me help. We'll face the Supreme Eltors together."

Evan laughed. "She's brave too, but so naïve."

"Do you trust him?" Scarlett asked me, ignoring Evan's comments.

"He is our best option. Please, trust me."

"Don't worry, I won't bite. There's absolutely nothing that would drive me to hurt you, or take anything from you." The darkness in Evan's smile returned. "And I think you'll find I'm the only one in this room who can say that."

"Stop it." Dru broke his silence. "We should go. This is getting ridiculous."

The Arca is right, for once. It's time to go, Kara added.

"You brought her this far without telling her the truth." There was no longer humor in Evan's demeanor.

"Enough." There was a new, stronger sense of authority in Dru's voice.

"She deserves to know everything. Unless you'd rather she did from someone else."

I felt the weight of Evan's threat, but it was Dru who responded, "We have no time."

"Of course you have time. They already know you're here. Don't tell me you honestly believe they're not connected with miss royalty over here," he said, pointing at Kara, who glared at him. Evan ignored her and continued. "They've got you exactly where they want you. All they're doing right now is waiting for you to come crawling into the Santrum."

Don't be absurd. We can't waste any more time just to humor the foolish Spark. Kara's voice was growing more impatient.

Unlike Dru, I'd gotten used to the echo of Kara's voice in my mind. I gave no physical indication Kara was speaking to me, but Evan said as though he knew, "Don't worry about the Agua. Tell the human."

I owed Scarlett the truth, but I also owed Dru and Kara the same, I thought. They stood with me in a Spark's cave after willingly going through unnecessary—and degrading—obstacles to help me. They, too, deserved to know the true extent of my betrayal.

"You owe Scarlett the truth. You can deal with"—he paused for a split second and glanced at the other two—"the rest another time."

He could read my mind.

The only thing that made it difficult to believe was he dared to invade an Astra's mind. Our brains were meant to keep infinite amount of information no other being, in all the worlds, should be able to cope with. For a second, I allowed a stream of profound information to float on the surface of my mind.

Evan stayed still until I stopped.

A second would have been harmless, but if he really was looking into my mind, it would show.

He grinned with an undeniable trace of satisfaction. "Are you just incapable of focusing on your priority? Shall we think of other ways to waste your time?"

He was right. We might have more time than we expected, but certainly not enough to spend trying to figure out the extent of a Spark's capability. After all, the Empyrs had spent millennia knowing very little about them for a reason.

"Good to know you haven't completely lost your mind. So, are you going to tell your precious friend all your *Forbidden* secrets?" Evan made it clear he was aware of the thought, the decision, that caused this whole predicament, but why was he more interested in urging me to tell Scarlett about the *Forbidden?*

"Well, put it this way, if she knew why having the chance to stay with me is the best thing that could happen to her in Empyrian, I'd have a more interesting time." He beamed as he responded to the question in my mind.

"Just tell me so he can shut up about it," Scarlett said. Once again, it was clear she wanted me to see there was nothing I, or anyone, could say that would change the way she felt about me. I wished I could believe she was right.

Evan must have caught my hesitation when I glanced at Kara and Dru. He offered a way to speak to Scarlett without being overheard by the other two. "You can tell her everything outside," he said, gesturing toward the door.

"You're not leaving us in here," Dru exclaimed, though his voice was weak. From his deteriorating posture, I could see he was beginning to feel the weight of the restricted space around him. "So what if we hear what you say? We're all in this together." He wouldn't be comfortable staying inside a Spark's confined cave, but that wasn't the reason he wanted to leave with us. There was eagerness in his tone. *He wanted to hear my confession,* I thought.

Before I could respond to Dru's comment, Kara's voice echoed in my mind. *The Arca has a point. Why do you need to be alone? What are you hiding?*

I couldn't respond to her question, which was enough to affirm I hadn't been completely honest.

I'm jeopardizing my place in my Corta for this. Kara's voice carried resentment so strong I felt the stab of every syllable.

"Do you really not get that it's not about you?" Evan addressed Kara. "A human jumped into an unknown world, ready to fight a battle she can't even begin to understand. I think she's earned a little privacy with her Astra, don't you?" Evan's tone was sharp.

Both Kara and Dru remained silent, evidently astounded by Evan's ability to respond to an Agua's unspoken sentiments.

As I took Scarlett's hand and led her to the door, Evan made a final remark. "Don't worry about keeping your voices down. These walls are thicker than they appear."

When we stepped out the door into a dark space, Scarlett grabbed my hand. She let out a short, nervous laugh when she realized we were walking through an ancient cave. "He made the inside of a cave look like my living room," she said, trying to highlight how ridiculous the act was, though unable to hide her admiration.

As we moved closer to the opening of the cave, the darkness began to fade, and something else caught Scarlett's attention. She bent down to touch the glimmering stones embedded on the ground. Her gaze followed the translucent wind slowly drifting up, and she gasped at the realization that the sky was even more radiant than the ground. Her eyes wandered with clear astonishment at how the colors—lilac, azure, and silver—blended into layers, tones, and shades she'd never seen before.

With every inch, every angle, she found something that dazzled her. Her eyes kept moving, refusing to stay focused, voracious to take everything in. Then, her gaze tumbled into the immense ocean before her.

"Incredible," Scarlett managed to say under a faint breath, "Your world."

"No. It's Evan's," I replied.

"Evan's?" she asked, without taking her eyes off the dense streaks of water that swiftly ascended and then gracefully spiraled back down into the ocean. Flying around the fluid spirals was a multitude of delicate spherical sea creatures. Thin, translucent fins were lined uniformly around its entire circumference. Each tantalizing fin emanated a different shade as it fanned back and forth, allowing the sphere figure to float around the spiral waves.

"Everything you see wasn't here before we entered the cave. In fact, this cave wasn't even down here." I exhaled a bitter sigh at the thought of the futile efforts for the unwarranted difficulties Evan had subjected us to.

"This isn't real? she asked and continued before I could reply. "My living room was in that cave. Of course, it isn't real." She spoke the last few words with a certain degree of severity, like she was trying to wake herself from a dream.

"It could be," I said carefully, trying, but failing, not to add to her confusion. "It's possible this is the true region of the Sparks. When we got here, we were unkindly received by the harsh environment. That was all Evan's doing, purely for his own entertainment. But this, the movement of the waves and how the water interacts with wind, it's far too graceful, far too effortless to be a product of manipulation."

"So, are you saying this is all real?"

"I'm saying that it could be, but that's not important right now. Scarlett, there is something you need to know. In fact, there are many things I haven't been brave enough to tell you."

"Why don't you start with what they really want from you?" Her tone matched the seriousness in mine.

"Do you remember the night I showed you who I really was?"

"Of course I do," she replied with a faint smile.

Had she been aware of how close I came to taking her life that night, she wouldn't have held the memory with such optimism.

"From the moment I met you, I wanted you to know me. That night, I had you in arms knowing you did. You accepted me. The happiness I felt was indescribable."

Emotion burned in her eyes, but she stayed silent, waiting for me to continue until her question had been answered.

I brushed my fingers over her cheek, attempting to soften her thoughtful expression. "I wanted to stay in that moment for eternity. I knew I needed to be with you for the rest of my life, but I also knew it wasn't possible, not when we're living in different time frames. Sooner than I could ever be prepared for, you'd be gone. Then I'd have to spend centuries without you. The thought of that brought fear for pain I wasn't sure I'd be able to control. Then I was certain. I couldn't, wouldn't, live without you. Not for a day, not a year, and definitely not for centuries. That was when I betrayed my kind."

"What did you do?"

"It was only a thought, and I had it for barely a moment, but my conviction to it was so strong they knew how certain I was."

"Petyr, please, just tell me."

"In that moment, I decided to live in your world, in your time—to become human."

"How?" she asked after a few seconds. She seemed to be battling with conflicted emotions.

"It wouldn't be an easy process, in fact it would be a long and painful one." I tried to say it in a lighthearted tone, but it didn't change Scarlett's somber expression. "I'd block parts of my brain and lose certain abilities. Subsequently, my heart would beat as fast as yours. I won't be strong enough to access and cultivate my Exir. I won't be able to live for much longer than you. I won't be able to jump much higher than you, or think much faster than you. I wouldn't know everything I do now."

"You wouldn't be you," she said with defeat.

She didn't seem to see how the transformation—which would render my physical attributes closer to hers—would break the barriers that separated us.

"Of course I'd still be me. I'd still feel the same. I'd love you with everything that I am, just as I do now." I tried to convince her, hoping she would realize my physical abilities were no longer the aspects that defined who I was.

Scarlett sighed and shook her head. "You'll be losing so much."

"But I'll be gaining so much more."

I wanted her to see, that to me, she was worth more than anything, but she ignored the implication of my response and said, "This is what they don't want to happen."

"That's why I have to face the Supreme Eltors. I have to see how far they're willing to go to ensure I stay the way I am. I'm not in danger. The only way they can hurt me is if you're there. This is why you have to stay with Evan."

She closed her eyes and nodded.

"You make everything sound so simple."

I heard Evan's voice as he stepped out of his cave. He'd witnessed an intimate conversation where I'd exposed just how far I'd fallen from the Astra I was. I couldn't say I was surprised he was listening. This was another way of letting us know we were still in his world, and he was still in control.

Scarlett glanced at Evan's direction. Though visibly offended by his intrusion, she seemed determined to ignore him. She found my eyes and locked them with hers, waiting for me to elaborate on Evan's statement.

I sighed. I was about to give her more reasons to worry. I had already given her so many. "Considering my position as an Eltor, my absence would be noticed in Empyrian. If everyone were to find out it was a possibility, a choice, to leave Empyrian and become something else . . ." I trailed off for a second as flashes of possible turmoil in my world dawned on me. "If they found out an Eltor had chosen to leave our world and become a weaker being, they'd start questioning our worth. Most wouldn't understand what I feel for you. Love, the kind that we have, it doesn't exist in my world, so they'd try to find a rational explanation. Eventually, they'd come to the conclusion that there could only be one reason why an Eltor would choose a more inferior state. They'd believe I decided to save myself because Empyrian was falling. Something like this could destroy, or at least change, our world. A world that generations of Supreme Eltors had worked very hard to preserve."

Scarlett appeared taken aback by this information. She hesitated for a moment, clearly astonished by the gravity a single choice could have on an entire world. Before I could remind her this was the result of my recklessness, I could see in her eyes she was already blaming herself. "You would risk ruining your world just to be with me." She was beginning to see me the way I had always been—selfish and irrational.

If I could help it, I'd stop everything. I'd go back to my old self, take my place as an Eltor, and forget about Scarlett. Nothing would be harmed, not our mission in the human world, not my fellow Eltors, not Empyrian, and certainly not Scarlett. If it were that simple, if I had the strength, I'd do it.

But even the brief thought of spending centuries without hearing her voice, seeing her smile, and feeling the warmth of her touch was so excruciating. I cringed at the sting it sent through my heart. The more I thought about the alternative, the more certain I was that being with her for the rest of my life was all I could ever do.

I tried to do the right thing. I tried to leave her, and it took all of my strength. But she didn't let me go. She found me. I owed it to her to try to find a way for us to be together. I could do it. I could think of a way. As long as I was confident she was safe, I could be my old self. I could think faster than anyone in the room. I could manipulate their thoughts. I'd get what I came for.

"Just," I said, repeating her word. I couldn't begin to explain the irreverence of using the word *just* to precede the possibility of being with her forever.

"If you think he's out of his mind now, wait 'till you hear the worst part," Evan interjected once again.

Scarlett's eyes were still fixed on mine, waiting for me to enlighten her. But this time, I couldn't. "All you need to know, for now, is that I will risk anything to be with you. I hope you understand this is no longer a choice for me. I need to be with you."

Scarlett threw a quick glance at Evan. She hesitated for a moment, clearly aware of his prying ears. She merely sighed and placed her arms around my neck, urging me closer. "Do whatever you need to do. I'll be here. There's nothing anyone can say that would make me run away."

"Are you sure, Scarlett? Can you . . . oh how do you humans put it?" Evan asked animatedly. He flashed a dark smile and continued, "Can you stomach it?"

Scarlett broke away from me and turned to Evan. "You wouldn't understand."

The smile on Evan's face vanished. "Petyr is risking your life right now as we speak, more than you can imagine. If he carries on the way he is, he'll be risking my life. That, I understand."

I held Scarlett closer, hoping my touch could shield her from the sting of the truth. She placed her hands on the sides of my face and whispered, "You know what you're doing." I could tell the reassurance was more for herself than for me, but I took it.

"If you're not up for telling her the rest, then let me do the honor." Evan addressed me this time.

"It's not your place," I protested.

"This is absolutely, undoubtedly my place." Evan tried to say his play on words lightheartedly, but he could no longer hide his genuine concern. He turned to Scarlett. "You know about the special attributes your Astra was lucky enough to be born with?"

She hesitated, but eventually nodded when she realized Evan wasn't going to let this go until he'd said his piece. I could see the pain in Scarlett's eyes as she thought of my abilities, once again reminding her of the magnitude of the distance between us.

"Having the potential to control every single element in any world, at any time, it's supposed to be the most guarded secret. The only thing he should have never told you. Aren't you going to ask why he shouldn't have told you?"

Scarlett didn't respond, but I could see a part of her wished I hadn't told her. Out of everything she found out about me, this was the one she had difficulty accepting. I wasn't just *different* anymore. I could tell somewhere in the back of her mind, she knew I wasn't only someone she couldn't be with, but someone she *shouldn't*.

"I'll tell you anyway." Evan seemed like he was about to flash his arrogant smile but couldn't bring himself to do so. It seemed his disappointment—and even fear—due to my poor judgment was beginning to melt his indifference. "It's a very dangerous secret because he's a very dangerous weapon. Keeping the *Shield* a secret is what keeps all the worlds secure."

"Enough," I finally managed.

Scarlett grew thoughtful. Even without the specific information, the history, she seemed to understand. But I could tell she wasn't willing to let it taint the trust she'd decided to place in me. "You know what you're doing," she repeated.

Scarlett had proven her commitment to me more times than she ever needed to. There were so many questions she could ask, so many objections, but she chose to trust me. Yet, I still couldn't bring myself to tell her what I should have long ago. I knew it didn't matter how much of my nature or ability I shared with her. As long as I kept her from knowing the *Forbidden*, every decision she made was based on deceit.

I had to confess. Evan had made it clear that if I didn't, he would tell her about the *Forbidden*. Scarlett had the right to hear it from me. I owed her that much. I had tried so many times to tell her the truth, but each time, I was overpowered by fear. Even now, I could feel the cruel hand of fear clasping my throat, paralyzing me. How would I begin to tell her the one thing I still struggled to accept? I pulled Scarlett into my arms, hoping my embrace would deflect her imminent revulsion. "There's more," a whisper was all I could manage. "There's one more thing you need to know."

"No, you have to focus on what you need to do right now. You'll have all the time you need to tell me everything when you get back."

"This is important. I should have told you—"

"Petyr," she interrupted. "Go. Come back. Then we'll talk."

X. FORBIDDEN

I was relieved for a brief moment before I felt the cold impact of dread from the secret that still hung on my shoulders. I should have insisted on telling her. Then, we'd both be free. I'd be free from the fear of not knowing if she could ever accept it, and she would be free from my deceit. But once again, Scarlett was right. This was no longer the time. My focus should now be on ensuring her safety. Not on being liberated from the fear and guilt I deserved.

Evan didn't urge me to dispute Scarlett's decision. Perhaps he, too, agreed with Scarlett. The reason didn't particularly matter to me. Taking advantage of his silence, I pulled Scarlett in my arms.

He waited for me to let go of Scarlett and face him, as if ensuring he had his audience's attention, before he moved. He held out his right palm and slowly closed it into a fist. With that motion, the cave behind us faded, leaving Dru and Kara in full view. Dru was hunched on the ground, his arms crossed on his knees, supporting his hooded head. I didn't have to see his expression to recognize his exasperation. After all, he was fighting a battle for someone who didn't even have the decency to be honest with him. I prepared myself to take Dru's accusations and even rage, but when he lifted his head up, he simply sighed and asked, "Are you finally ready?"

Unlike Dru, Kara's fists were clenched as if trying to keep her sentiments from reaching her face. But just beneath the hard surface, I could see a myriad of emotions—the uncertainty, frustration, humiliation, anger, regret, and doubt—fighting their way through her unsympathetic façade. In spite of her very nature, she allowed herself to feel compassion. After essentially betraying her Supreme Eltors by coming to my aid, she'd ended up trapped in a Spark's cave whilst I kept her in the dark. When she heard Dru's voice, uncertainty materialized in the slight crease between her eyebrows. Only for a brief second, then she was back. Neither commitment nor compassion brought her back to focus. It was an Agua's pride. I could pinpoint the moment when she decided to ensure she didn't appear defeated by an Arca's apparent ability to control his emotions.

Kara closed her eyes for a second, took a deep breath, and said in a controlled voice that equaled Dru's, "Jump. I'll be right behind you."

I pulled Scarlett in my arms one last time, and then, without allowing myself to hesitate, I jumped. I kept my senses focused on Scarlett's location, but I couldn't hear her or detect her in any way. I knew she was safe with Evan, but I couldn't seem to get myself to let go. Evan must have expected this as it didn't take long—just long enough for him to know I'd covered too much distance to risk turning back—before I heard his voice.

You just can't help yourself, can you?

He was pushing his words to me, but not in my mind, not the way an Agua would. It was merely an isolated sound directed toward me, meant only for me to hear. In that same instant, I should have chosen not to hear anymore. I should have blocked their location off my hearing range without a second thought. Hearing Scarlett's voice wouldn't be a good idea. I needed to distance myself from her to ensure I could exude a sense of indifference when they asked me about her. My curiosity for Evan's motives kept me holding for a few seconds too long, and then it was too late.

Has anyone told you about Felix?

I froze.

A volt of shame struck my body, making it far too weak to move, let alone jump. I considered turning back, but I knew I was too far away to make it to Scarlett in time. I could feel Dru and Kara slowing down, almost to a halt, but I didn't move. I kept listening, waiting.

Evan wouldn't show allegiance to the Supreme Eltors and the very system that had degraded his kind for centuries, but I knew he wasn't on my side either. His intention wasn't to help me, but to prove he could do whatever he wanted for his own amusement, and it wasn't in my power to stop him.

In your world, you have technology to get from one country to another, but here we have the passages. You remember using one to get here? There are many others, but still not enough to cover everything. Sometimes, we have to take an exit to the human world, and then jump into another one from there. That's what Felix was doing.

I stopped listening. I blocked the sounds and wielded myself to focus on making my way to the Supreme Eltors, but his voice found me again.

He heard a scream.

Evan must have realized I had stopped listening from their location and moved, so he could continue pushing his words to me. It wasn't enough that I knew Scarlett would learn my most shameful secret. No. He wanted me to hear the words I was too afraid to say. There was no escaping it. I had to face it, but I couldn't let it break me. I needed to be the Astra I was, now more than ever. I tried to find some form of logic. I considered the possibility that it was all still a trick. Perhaps, he wasn't speaking to Scarlett. *This was just another maneuver to distract me from my objective,* I thought.

Then I heard Scarlett's soft voice.

What did he do?

Her question brought the images I had been trying to push away, back to the forefront of my mind. But none of it compelled me to lose focus and turn back. Each image was a reminder of why I should keep going. This was one of the many times when Scarlett had provided me with unexpected strength, saving me from my own weakness.

Empyrs are not supposed to interfere with the humans. But Felix was an Astra, and his curiosity got the better of him.

I knew his last words were aimed to aggravate me, but they were powerless. Each time I jumped, the wind rushed to my comfort. I was becoming closer to the Astra I used to be.

He came across a human, about to be attacked by a wild animal.

Evan's voice was still clear when it reached me, but the wind had extinguished the impact of his words.

The human had been running. It was pointless, of course. It didn't take too long before he ran out of energy and courage, and he was on the ground. He was so spent and afraid. His heart was beating so hard and fast like it was building up to an explosion.

Every Empyr knew this story, but it wasn't often told. In fact, most would go out of their way to avoid hearing it again. Empyrs didn't like to be reminded of their weakness, and most would still rather believe they didn't have any. Some refused to acknowledge the story of Felix because they claimed what happened to him was a mere result of his own personal weakness. It didn't reflect our entire race. Alas, this was nothing more than a feeble denial of the truth we all knew.

The human's heart seemed to beat faster and louder until Felix could hear no other sound. It no longer mattered who he was and why he was there. He was overcome by the invigorating sensation that pulled him closer to the human, to the sound. He couldn't resist it. He didn't want to resist it. He didn't know how he got to that state, which for an Astra, was an impossibility.

Evan told the story with such ease only a Spark could manage. Despite the fact that most Empyrs chose to believe they would never be weak enough to be affected by the sound of a human's heartbeat, the threat that no one could truly understand brought fear that my kind wasn't used to.

The closer he got to it, the more enticing it became. His Exir radiated, almost unable to contain itself with every beat that sent a rush of blood through the human's veins.

I allowed myself nothing more than a subtle flinch at the memory of the very sensation I had experienced—more than once—with Scarlett. The moments in her bedroom, the night I confessed my identity to her, and all the other times I was almost tempted by the sound of her heartbeat. Each came with a bitter pang. Even a Spark's uninhibited account couldn't, with true accuracy, portray the euphoria and the intoxication and the excruciating desire.

He extended his hand and placed his palm on the human's chest. He stayed still for a few seconds, indulging himself to drown in the sound of the human life. At this point, he claimed he was something else entirely. His Exir had taken over him, but every inch of his Nherum form could feel the immeasurable pleasure.

This was it. Evan's next few words would allow Scarlett to recognize her close encounters with the *Forbidden*. She would remember all the moments when I extended my hand to her chest, and she would realize this wasn't a simple expression of affection. I jumped higher. Faster. Wind was my fortress, pressing hard against my skin, preventing even a ripple of uncalculated movement. I knew it would take less than a flinch of emotion for me to fall apart. I focused on encasing myself with a strong exterior, not allowing myself to feel, to react.

Felix's fingers slowly sank into the human's feeble skin, breaking through brittle bones. He stopped only when he felt the viscid crust of the flesh. It pressed up onto the tip of his fingers for the briefest instant before retreating back with every faint beat.

His voice lingered on every syllable giving Scarlett—and me—enough time to envisage every brutal detail. Beneath his solemn demeanor was an air that mocked me. His tone that mimicked mine uttered the words I couldn't say.

The Exir inside him was blazing. Hungry. But he was calm. The blood that seeped through the human's wounded flesh held Felix steady as it glided through the spaces between his fingers, down the back of his hand, keeping him connected to the very muscle that pushed its flow. The heart, his to take. As he withdrew it—so delicately—out of the lifeless body, to his face, he was no longer separated from his Exir. He became more than just a vessel that incubated the Exir until it was strong enough to desert him. His Exir had woven itself into his veins, muscles, tissues, bones . . . until his skin felt with it, and its sound echoed in his own mind, harmonized with his own voice.

As he described the way Felix lost himself, it was difficult to overlook how Evan, too, was no longer himself. He had taken the role of a storyteller, faithful to the details, and stripped of his typical condescending judgments. His monotonous voice willed me to focus on the images he conjured up and feel Felix's experience.

Then, the human heart no longer felt like raw tender flesh, but a sensation. It was elation, comfort, thrill, bliss, and ecstasy all wrapped in one sublime sensation in the palm of Felix's hand. He fixed his gaze at it—guarding it with such zeal, like it was the most precious thing in all the worlds—as it gradually disintegrated into his pores. Every splinter of the heart he absorbed gave a shot of the sensation that overtook his body. He relished every fragment until there was nothing left. And then, he became irrevocably changed.

Silence followed the end of Evan's story. I wasn't to know Scarlett's reaction. But that wasn't the end of Felix. He came back to Empyrian to tell his story, with precise detail that was very close to Evan's execution. Felix was proud of what he had achieved. *A higher existence and clarity*, he called it, as he boasted a resilient Exir that would have taken him centuries to attain. Everyone was intrigued. They believed this discovery could be an efficient way to further strengthen our kind. Our Exirs would develop and mature faster, saving centuries in the process of reproduction. However, the Supreme Eltors were not convinced. In our history, generations of leaders had tried every possible way of living until they found the most effective method. One of the Supreme Eltors' responsibilities was to preserve this system. It was understandable, therefore, that any threat of change, irrespective of how optimistic it may seem, wasn't taken lightly.

The Supreme Eltors didn't have time to deliberate for much longer as the change in Felix's physical form manifested. Just like Alex in the woods, Felix kept his elation. Even as his decomposing skin rotted on his bones, he never once showed regret. The more optimistic Empyrs considered the possibility that the death of Felix's Nherum form was being sped up because his Exir was ready to move on to a higher realm.

When Felix's Exir exploded, there was a resounding certainty. The human heart was a lethal threat—an overwhelming and irresistible threat. This was the reason the Eltors were sent to the human world, to find answers. As I thought of Felix's story, without the aid of Evan, I knew I was no longer afraid.

He wants to steal your heart. Not in a good way.

Evan's voice was back to his usual condescending tone. His final push to see if I could still break. But my fortitude was solid. I didn't resent Evan for telling the story. In fact, the only emotion close to the surface was a sense of relief, and I let it wash through me for a while. The secret that had been tormenting me was out. I was free. Scarlett's love was strong, and maybe it could withstand this. If it couldn't, then, at least it would be her honest choice. Right now, my single priority was to guarantee her safety.

You face your fears, then you have nothing to be afraid of.

Evan's final words hung in my mind as I made the rest of my journey to the Santrum. There was something quite obscure in those words, not in meaning but in motivation. His scornful tone, even at its best, couldn't cover the distinct sincerity. As long as I had Scarlett in my life, I'd never run out of fears. I'd always be weak. But right now I didn't feel afraid. Evan held me down and forced my eyes open, liberating me from the overriding darkness that crippled my senses. All those fears were now so distant, irrelevant. Irrespective of his intentions, I couldn't deny Evan helped me restore the appearance of the Astra I was.

With every jump, I regained my old agility and strength. When I reached the shore, I knew Dru and Kara were still a few seconds behind. I stood in front of Lenara, a vast silver ocean. Not even an Eltor's eyes could trace its end. The water was heavy—still, potent, and calculating. It wasn't here to thrash uninhibitedly and dance with the wind. It was a formidable sentinel surrounding the Santrum.

Let's go in. The Arca can find his own way.

Kara's voice sprung in my mind with severity. It seemed I wasn't the only one who planned to show the Supreme Eltors that the human world couldn't change us.

"We'll wait."

Pathetic. Speed was the one thing he had going for him.

I didn't respond to Kara's slur as I could already hear Dru closing in. When he arrived, I only had time to give him a quick glance before Kara nudged me toward the Lenara. Dru's face was tucked in the shadow of his hood, but his bearing accentuated his exhaustion. He kept his human clothes on, including his gloves and his shoes, which prevented him from connecting with the elements of nature that would have enriched his physical power. With both Kara and I also in our human clothing, it certainly gave a sense of unity. An effective way of reminding the Supreme Eltors of our commitment to our mission.

We stepped closer to the water and, for a split second, leaned forward to touch it with the tip of our fingers. Then, we waited. The Santrum was a second home to Eltors. This was where we were cultivated to develop the skills and understanding of the responsibilities that came with our position, preparing us to one day take the place of the Supreme Eltors. We had made this trip many times before, but somehow I felt as though we were about to enter an unfamiliar territory.

We stayed very still as the water began to circle around each of us, swiftly forming into three translucent cylinders that rose up to the base of our necks. I held my breath just before the one enclosing me pressed onto my skin. It took hold of my torso in a firm grip, the Lenara's way of checking for genetic evidence that we were entitled to enter the Santrum. This place was open only to Eltors and, occasionally, certain Empyrs authorized by a Supreme Eltor.

The Lenara provided a steadfast, impenetrable security for the Santrum. It wouldn't be possible for me to simply jump or even for Kara to swim toward it. The Santrum wasn't only shielded—as the water could turn solid in an instant, destroying any unwarranted intruders—but it also moved constantly within the Lenara, making it undetectable.

I had entered this place thousands of times before without even giving it a second thought, but this time, I didn't feel the same sense of entitlement. I was very much aware I was no longer the same Eltor that the Lenara welcomed for centuries. My recent choices were bound to leave marks of the irrevocable change, etched beneath my skin. Somewhere in the back of my mind, I heard an irrational voice wonder, *Will I be allowed in?*

The Lenara's water didn't feel liquid against my skin. Warm and flexible, it clung to me like rubber. Once we were released from its grip, the water descended to our feet. It lifted us up, and we slid down the surface of the wave, and then another, surfing to the opening of the Santrum. Just as swiftly as the vigorous waves formed around us, the water descended and retreated back into the ocean, leaving the three of us standing just outside the colossal wall of frozen sea water that enclosed the Santrum. Both the wall and the water were thousands of feet in height, but there were merely five feet of space between them. No gates or doors on the wall that encircled the Santrum. Any intruder who had made it this close to the Santrum would have very little chance of actually getting in or going back to safety. The Lenara's water surrounding the wall would swallow anyone who was ignorant enough to swim to the shore.

For Eltors, however, we only had to press our palms against any part of the wall, and the impenetrable matter would transform into a soft veil. Only Eltors and Supreme Eltors had the ability to do this, which meant anyone with permission to enter must be met outside the wall.

The Santrum itself was vast enough to accommodate areas for the three Cortas. Either due to old habits or sheer longing for a place that could offer us even the faintest sense of belongingness, the moment we stepped into the Santrum, our eyes fell onto our Cortas' spaces.

Mine was straight ahead. Visible, though far enough that it would take me at least five jumps to reach it. Resembling a part of the Astran region, Celestria, it was elevated and rested above a thick layer of lavender and silver fog. Of course, the imitation didn't come close to the magnificence that resided above the skies, but it was a sufficient accommodation during our time in the Santrum. Though smaller, the Astran shelters in the Santrum had the same roofless octagonal shape. The open space allowed us to connect with the immense body of celestial elements, of which an adequate imitation was also projected above each dwelling space.

Apart from serving as a place for the Astran Eltors to stay whilst in the Santrum, its main purpose was to allow the Eltors from the other Cortas to gain better understanding of the Astran culture. Though it was accepted that the understanding of nature and ways of all three Cortas was imperative for Eltors, no one was prepared to give much more than the basics. After all, it was the boundaries and knowing there were so much more behind those barriers that kept Empyrian balanced.

Dru's eyes were fixed to the left side of the Santrum. The long stretch of vast and uniformed trees emulated the Great Evrass, except here, there were no shadows to conceal what's inside. We could see the thicker trees that housed the Arcas. Each had an inconspicuous entrance within the large roots. These led down to a much larger space underneath, to the place where the Arcas were most comfortable. Where they were closest to the heart of Earth, the life source of everything that sprung from nature. These spaces were almost bare, but I wouldn't imagine them to be so in the real region of the Arca.

Across from the Arcan region stood the Aguan still lake, Sevrin. This had always been my least preferred place in the Santrum. I didn't go there unless parts of our training required me to do so. It was bright and mesmerizing, sparkling against the sunshine. A castle made of clear, frozen water floated in the middle of Lake Sevrin. This, too, had a distinct radiance. Though the thickness of the walls made them less transparent, it was the brilliant reflection that deflected anyone from seeing through the translucent walls. Like the Arcan dwelling spaces, there was also nothing but empty rooms inside the Aguan castle. The Agua's space was beautiful, but there was something unattractive about it: cold and empty.

All three regions were fluidly fused to each other—tremendous in their difference, yet one.

Dru was the first to turn away from the reminder of his home. Kara and I followed, and we all made our way to face the Supreme Eltors. We didn't run or jump or do anything to hasten the final stretch of our journey.

We all knew exactly where the Supreme Eltors would be: the Lyceum. The most sacred place in the Santrum, the one that held the history—and the secrets—of our world.

Only one way existed to get to the Lyceum. Through the well. Unlike the Supreme Eltors who had the ability to summon the well, we hadn't yet been granted open access to the Lyceum. Though, on occasion, we'd notice the well appear—often in inconspicuous and isolated places—it would vanish before any of us could satisfy our curiosity. This time, however, the well materialized right in the middle of the Santrum. The opening was surrounded by piles of ancient rocks, creating four feet of resilient fortification. On it, a single rope made of thick, gold threads hung artlessly. The shaft gave the impression of immense depth. No water was visible, just complete blackness.

Kara stepped forward and placed her hand on the golden rope. We all knew how it worked, but none of us had used it without the aid of a Supreme Eltor. Kara's uncertainty was apparent from the way her fingers lingered on the rope just a few seconds too long before she finally clasped it in her hand.

Dru and I stood in complete silence as we watched Kara pull the rope from the well. Her eyes fixed on the part of the rope that dropped down into the well, almost as if expecting to see the other end with each vigorous pull. She exhaled a flutter of relief when she saw water rising up and stopped when it was close enough to the surface of the surrounding rocks. She climbed up and stepped in the middle of the well. For a full second, she stood on the water as though she was on solid ground. Then she disappeared into it. The water was swift as it descended into the dark empty hole.

"Can I go?" Dru asked, his voice even weaker now that we were moments away from facing the Supreme Eltors.

They would know Dru stayed by my side as I struggled to understand my erratic emotions. He chose to help me. He didn't leave my side, not even now that I faced an uncertain future. What would that make him in the eyes of the Supreme Eltors? Would they consider his loyalty to me as betrayal?

Why did he ask to go before me? Was it to reassure me he wasn't afraid? Was it because he didn't trust himself to go through with it alone? Whatever the reason, it shouldn't matter. I should tell him not to go at all. He should head back to his home, the Great Evrass. His absence would send the message he didn't approve of my actions. This was my final chance to be a reasonable friend. I shouldn't let him be punished for my decisions.

I spoke without meeting his eyes. "Dru, I don't think you should go. One way or another, they'll punish me. If they see you by my side, they might—"

"They don't have anything they can use to hurt me," he said coldly.

He was right. I was the only one with weakness.

Without another word, Dru picked up the golden rope and began to pull. This time, soil rose up the well. Dru disappeared into it, just as Kara did. When it was my turn, wind ascended from the depths of the well, moving in circular motion. The wind was fast enough to be visible, yet soft and calm, not threatening like the waves of Lenara. I could feel the wind below my feet as I stood in the middle of the well. I was pulled down, and in an instant, I was inside the Lyceum.

Albeit enclosed and sheltered, the Lyceum was spacious enough to accommodate all the Supreme Eltors and Eltors at any given time without causing discomfort. The floor was made of the rarest rocks and cosmic gemstones only the most skilled Astras could acquire, woven into intricate patterns under a smooth and evenly polished surface. The walls and the high ceiling were made of frozen water. Though comparably radiant, these were not translucent like the Aguan castle. Within the walls were thousands of boxes, securely held by vines and branches.

On the surface, these boxes appeared to be made of simple dark metal, but with a closer look, any Empyr would realize it was forged with some of the rarest and most resilient elements. The Midnight Pearls that lined the surface could only be found in the most erratic and severe part of the deep. The Titryian Gold was excavated only by the most skilled Arcas. The indestructible Etherist Stone that sealed the edges of the boxes could only be attained by an Astra who was capable of traveling across seven layers of universes, through a passage into the world of Sinteria. The boxes were made to withstand time, fire, force, and any other possible means of destruction. Each held vital secrets of our kind.

Kara, Dru, and I were at the center of the Lyceum. The Supreme Eltors stood on elevated platforms around us. Within my immediate view was Kalista, an Agua whose fierce blue eyes demanded to hold my gaze. She used to remind me of Kara—before I truly knew Kara. They both always wore blue robes made of threads from the floras and minerals of the deep, with such elegance that the fabric seemed more lustrous and the patterns more intricate than they should be. The resemblance was always obvious from the impeccable stream of their long radiant blonde hair, to the sense of authority in their poise. The similarities still remained, but it now seemed mindless to compare the two. Kara wasn't the callous Agua we thought she was. No, she was nothing like Kalista. I broke free from Kalista's gaze sooner than she expected me to dare. I had never been afraid of her, and she needed to know it hadn't changed.

I turned my attention to the podium next to hers. Another Agua, Rex, stood with equal sense of regency. Unlike Kalista, however, Rex's eyes didn't command my attention. He spoke more often than any Agua I'd known. His voice was always steady and indifferent, his facial expressions guarded. Rex found the fine line between courtesy and pretense, and he stood right in the middle of it. He would never be as skilled as an Astra in this particular game, but he was good at it, good enough that I didn't always find him easy to read. I gave him a faint smile and single nod before turning away, a simple gesture meant to unsettle him.

Edmeer, an Arca and the oldest Supreme Eltor, held a more welcoming expression. His Nherum form was frail, but he had the strongest Exir in Empyrian. This made him far wiser, calmer, and more controlled. This also meant he was close to the end. When the time came for him to release his Exir, Dru would take his place as a Supreme Eltor. Perhaps, this was why Dru wasn't afraid. At least in the near future, they'd need him more than they'd need me.

On the podium next to Edmeer's were Ellaya and Leera. All three Arcan Supreme Eltors had the same dark hair, wild eyes, and bare feet. They wore shorts and sleeveless garments made of threads from durable mineral and herbal sources. They all exuded such compassion and warmth only an Arca could, but there was a visibly uncharacteristic caution in Ellaya's manner. The first confirmation that the Supreme Eltors' plan included something far more vicious than an Arca's conscience could take lightly. *They intended to kill.*

"I'm glad you came back. I knew you couldn't just walk away from us." Leera spoke with ardency in her voice. I relished the sight of innocence in her beaming face. It was clear she had no knowledge of the Supreme Eltors' intentions. I returned her smile as I reminded myself that Scarlett was safe. *She was with a Spark, out of the Supreme Eltors' reach.*

With the thought of Scarlett, I couldn't help but picture her reaction if she were to see Leera's true Nherum form. I wondered if she would believe that the youngest Eltor, looking no older than a seven-year-old human child, with windswept hair and artless gestures, was the same individual who appeared to us with such grace and elegance. I wondered how she would react. Before I could allow my façade to melt into the pleasure of thinking about Scarlett, I willed myself to focus my attention on the two remaining Supreme Eltors. The Astras.

Harper and Oswald were similar in many ways. They both wore the same lightweight trousers and vest made with threads from rare celestial minerals that sung with the wind. They had the same shades of red in their brown hair, inquisitive green eyes, and impeccable control of their posture and expressions. They were equally rational, and they had always stood unequivocally loyal to our Corta. I was therefore curious to see they had chosen not to uphold a united front. Harper was in position just as the other Supreme Eltors, but Oswald's podium was empty. He'd chosen to stand on the lower ground, leaning on the wall behind his supposed pedestal. His role as a Supreme Eltor compelled him to stay with the others, but his refusal to stand with them inflicted a chink in their impenetrable armor. I felt an immediate sense of camaraderie when my eyes fell on Oswald, even before he spoke.

"Don't worry, Petyr, I won't be a part of the interrogation committee. You have my trust and loyalty, and Harper should pledge the same."

"I haven't turned my back on him, but I have a responsibility to maintain, and so do you," Harper said calmly. He gave me a reassuring nod, which I took as a subtle promise he was still on my side.

"What is that responsibility, exactly? Pretending to ask questions you already know the answers to?" Oswald raised his voice, directing his question to the rest of the Supreme Eltors.

I responded before any of them could. I couldn't afford to waste any more time. "There are certain things only I can answer. Ask me anything. I have nothing to hide," I declared with the composure and confidence of a true Astra.

Don't you? Kalista's severe voice struck my mind. The callous sound matched the coldness in her eyes. Both were aimed to weaken me, but not enough to break my confidence.

"Kalista, we agreed you'd speak. For the sake of fair judgment, it is imperative everyone has the same amount of information," Edmeer stated.

Kalista hesitated for a moment, and then she addressed me with spoken words. "Why don't you enlighten us about your rather close encounters with the *Forbidden*?"

"I'm still here, with my Exir perfectly intact. I believe that speaks for itself. Unless, you need more explanation to help your understanding?" A subtle insult to their intelligence was always an effective way to get under an Agua's skin.

Perhaps to prevent any further incivility, Harper spoke before Kalista could retaliate. "Indeed, it showed remarkable control on your part."

"You were merely a couple of breaths away from ripping the human's beating heart out of her chest." The agonizing truth in Kalista's words was a familiar one. I had punished myself with the image of it in my mind many times before. I battled to keep my composure. She wasn't going to break me with her brutal words. She wasn't going to win.

When she realized I wouldn't give her the confirmation she needed, she turned to Kara. "I felt it when you did. Tell us what the Astra is trying so hard to conceal, Kara."

This was Kara's chance to prove her loyalty to her Corta. She tried to speak with her usual poise and confidence, but the strain in her voice conveyed that she remained conflicted as to where her allegiance laid. "Yes, I felt his submission. In that moment when he allowed himself to get lost in the sensation, I felt the darkness of his future, as well as the future of Empyrian."

"See—" Kalista began her victorious roar.

"But, he had already resisted the *Forbidden* before I got to him," Kara interrupted. She continued before Kalista could say anymore. "He didn't need my help. He was strong enough to break free from the hold of the *Forbidden*, and he had proven it more than once."

"You disappoint me. I look at you and I don't see an Agua. I see only weakness and foolishness." She tried to sound disappointed and almost saddened, but there was a resounding threat in her tone.

"Securing an Agua on your side, impressive. You must be the first one to resist the *Forbidden*, but that's a definite achievement," Oswald said in a lighthearted manner, but I sensed the compliment was genuine.

"Kara has made a valid point," Ellaya responded, ignoring Oswald's comment.

Leera beamed as her Supreme Eltor spoke.

In spite of Kalista's venomous gaze, Ellaya continued, "Petyr did manage to resist the *Forbidden*. This is something we should consider, instead of wasting time either pressing him to admit his mistakes, or waiting for inconsistencies in his statements. After all, he is still an Astra. He is still capable of concealing what he doesn't want us to see."

"Ellaya is right," Harper said in an even tone, "Resisting the *Forbidden* was something we had expected to be impossible. The young Eltors were sent to the human world to gain a deeper understanding of the humans, in the aim to learn the causes of the Exir's attraction to the human heart. His experience had been perilous, yes, but we can't deny its value. From this, we know there is a way for us to resist our only weakness. All we need now is to find out exactly how, and then the Empyrs will once again be completely fearless and unspoiled."

Edmeer was thoughtful as he nodded in agreement. When he spoke, his voice was soothing, more sincere than Harper's. "We can't question the value of the young Astra's experiences. However, this doesn't change the fact that he has committed a deplorable sin. He has consciously chosen to turn his back on his kind as well as his duties. He has chosen to become human."

Beside me, I could feel Kara stiffen as she was reminded of the weight of my betrayal, that I didn't deserve her loyalty.

"It was an insignificant thought I entertained for less than an instant. I hadn't committed to anything. There is no sin," I protested, though I knew it would be futile. The Supreme Eltors would have felt the level of my conviction to the thought, growing stronger as I got closer to Scarlett.

Rex ignored my appeal. He said, monotonous and expressionless, "You should know better, Kalista. It is certainly not wise to try to outwit an Astra. He will have a reason, an explanation for everything. Therefore, let me say it plainly. The human girl will die."

Before I could, Kara spoke in defense of Scarlett. "She is not a threat, no more than any other human. She can help us understand. Tell them, Dru. Say something."

I was in complete awe of Kara's integrity—despite my betrayal.

In Dru's silence, Ellaya cried, "We're not killers. This is not what we do."

"No, we're not killers, but we're creatures of survival. We have always been resilient and rational. We do what we have to." Edmeer maintained his calmness as he explained.

"You're all willing to taint our hands with blood of the helpless. For what reason? The possibility that one of us might use his free will?" Oswald managed to keep his voice steady, but I—and I'm sure Harper—could detect the thick anger beneath it.

"She knows what we are. Petyr had her killed the moment he released his Exir in front of the human," Kalista said, finally breaking her temporary silence.

Though his face remained expressionless, Rex's fierce gaze held mine. "She made you weak, willed you to fall. You exposed us. You're willing to betray your kind and your destiny, all for a human. She cannot, will not live." I fought very hard to keep calm as Rex uttered the words that convicted Scarlett to death. I reminded myself again and again that Scarlett was safe. I almost believed it, but then Rex added, "Worse of all, you risked an Empyr's life by bringing the very weakness of every Exir into our world."

No.

They knew. Of course, they knew.

I tried to convince myself that even though they knew Scarlett was in Empyrian, Aris wouldn't find her. They wouldn't be able to trace Evan.

"Harper," I said as firmly as I could. The distinct tone that pleaded for help was meant only for Harper and Oswald to hear.

He shook his head. "I agree with them, Petyr." Harper was solemn when he continued, "It is the most rational solution. We need to *erase* her because we need you. Her family will forget. It will be a clean death. She will not suffer."

"A clean death? Is that supposed to convince me? Am I supposed to hold my hands up and give in to your judgment?" The rising tone of threat in my last words wasn't limited to the Astras' ears. "I won't let you kill her."

"Why are you fighting so hard to protect this human?" Edmeer sounded more curious than critical. The question seemed so senseless that it angered me. Scarlett meant more to me than anything in all the worlds, and protecting her from individuals who were determined to kill her was as natural as a reflex, a heartbeat. Alas, there was nothing I could say, no information in the thousands of the ancient boxes in the walls of the Lyceum would help them understand what I felt.

"You don't have to answer that. We can just see for ourselves." Anticipation replaced the hostility in Kalista's face. She closed her eyes and continued, "I can feel him. He's close."

I knew she meant Aris. I hoped he was alone. He couldn't have found Scarlett. *As long as she's with Evan, she's untraceable*, I reminded myself.

She is safe. She is safe. She is safe. I repeated the words in my mind to keep my confidence from falling apart. I was determined to keep my breathing steady and show no sign of anxiety as Aris materialized, alone, in front of the Aguas' podiums.

When Evan appeared behind him clutching Scarlett's arm, I lost my breath.

My façade shattered. I no longer cared if I had lost the appearance of the self-possessed Astra. All I wanted to do was to pull her from Evan's tight grip and take her as far away from here as possible. I bent my knees, preparing to jump when Evan spoke. "Are you sure you want to jump? Can't you feel that? The wind within these walls is not on your side."

He was right. The wind was heavy and unnatural, an evident part of the Lenara. I was even more helpless than I'd anticipated. My body trembled and my voice was coarse as I screamed, "Get your hands off her! If anyone hurts a single hair on her body, I will—"

"Do what?" Aris had the quintessential look of an Agua—from his elegant attire, to his pristine golden hair, ruthless blue eyes, and arrogant composure. Except this time, he stood with a heavier air of menace beside the two trophies that signified his victory. He'd captured the Spark and the human. His face was filled with sheer pleasure at the sight of the fallen Astra. "You would rebel and betray your kind? You'd place your world in jeopardy? You have already done all those things. What is left to satisfy that sweet revenge? Harm your Supreme Eltors, perhaps?"

"No. He isn't foolish enough to think he could harm his Supreme Eltors." Edmeer answered before I could respond. "However, there's one thing I know he's considering. If we kill the human, he would extinguish his Exir and kill his Nherum form. We would lose not only an Eltor, but the *Shield*." Edmeer's statement almost took me by surprise. There was no sign of resentment or accusation in his demeanor. In fact, apart from Aris and Kalista, no one else seemed to revel at the sight of my weakness. Whilst Rex remained expressionless, Leera's eyes were wide in sorrow, and Ellaya was unable to hide her concern. Harper kept his composure, but allowed me to see the compassion hindered by a hint of disappointment in his eyes, something I had seen too many times in Nero's.

Oswald's disappointment was more apparent. On the surface, he kept an air of nonchalance, but it was only too obvious to me he had lost most of his confidence. He could barely stand the sight of a trembling Astra, with emotions spilled and thoughts exposed for even an Arca to read. It seemed he was already mourning my loss. Everyone knew I was charging at a battle I could never win. Even the Spark looked at me with pity.

I wondered what Scarlett was thinking, feeling. I hadn't had the strength to look at her directly. Would her eyes that had held me with reverence now bear resentment for putting her life in danger? Would there be regret for placing so much trust in someone who was unable to protect her? Would there be blame for all my poor decisions and dishonesty? Would there be disgust for knowing what I was capable of? Would there still be love?

I had but one last bullet to fire. I was the *Shield*. I could control any element in any world, and any world would crumble at my will. It was time to let them consider the magnitude of the destruction someone who had nothing more to live for, or to be afraid of, could cause. "No, I won't kill myself. That would be too easy, too kind."

"Don't be stupid. Have you not been paying attention? Most of them would rather not kill her, and that threat you have in mind would only convince them to do so. You're desperate, but you're not stupid."

I froze at the sound of the voice.

No.

"Finally." Evan sighed in relief and continued in his typical cool tone. "I was honestly beginning to think you'd never speak, and my plan really depended on you speaking."

How could Evan have known? It couldn't possibly be! No. It must be a mistake. There must be another explanation for the calmness, that bitter calmness I'd heard more times than I could bear. The same sound rang in my mind as I recalled Alex's voice, moments before he perished in the woods.

No. Not now. Not Dru.

"Well, I might as well get rid of these," Dru said as he took off his gloves and hood, exposing what's left of the putrid skin on the moldering bones of his hands and scalp. "They're starting to feel unbearably heavy."

"Dru! No! No! No! Not you!" A hysterical cry exploded from Leera. Though both Ellaya and Edmeer remained silent, the pain and fear in their faces were undeniable. Harper and Oswald were also silent, but unlike the shock and disgust on Aris's face, their eyes were more observant, taking in every last detail of Dru's appearance.

"I expected nothing more from such weak Exir," Kalista attempted to recover from failing to discern Dru's tragic fate. Everyone, including Rex whose apathetic face was also fixed on Dru, ignored her.

"How dare you!" Kara exclaimed, only slightly more restrained than Leera's frantic manner. "How dare you be so weak! I should have known. I felt it. I felt something on the way to the passage. I should have known it was you!" I could tell she was hurt more than angry. She cared about Dru, more than any of us had realized. From the pain in her tone, it was evident she blamed herself for not paying enough attention to recognize Dru's condition, but this wasn't her fault. It was mine. If everyone's attention wasn't focused on me, we could have saved Dru before he committed the *Forbidden.*

I failed to acknowledge it in the woods when Alex pointed at Dru and uttered words of warning, and again with the ominous sense of dread both Kara and I felt as we made our way to the passage. The signs were all there, screaming for my attention—his weakened voice, the change in his temperament, his refusal to touch a tree or enter the Great Evrass. How could I have ignored the obscurity of his choice to run with his shoes on? How could I have let this happen to him?

"I did this to you. I'm sorry." I uttered a feeble apology, but the sound of my pain clung to each syllable.

"That's your problem. You give yourself too much credit. This has nothing to do with you. Sometimes, things are simply meant to happen."

Dru's serenity was haunting. Despite his statement, violent guilt thrashed in my chest. I was about to watch the agonizing death of the one person who hadn't forsaken me. Guilt and pain weighed me down until I could no longer bear to stand.

"You don't know what you're talking about. I can save you!" Leera started to run toward Dru, ready to give him her blood, but Ellaya held her back. "It will kill you, Leera. You're too young. I will do it."

Kalista gasped in disgust, but before she could say anything, Dru and Edmeer spoke in unison. "No."

"It is too late," Edmeer added, bitterness was palpable in his somber tone.

"It has been too late before it even began. It's even too late for you." Dru struggled to lift his head to face me. "Let go. Stop punishing yourself. Everything that is weighing you down, everything you think matters, doesn't. What are you holding on to? You're not in love. It's an illusion, and a part of you knows that."

"You're wrong." I struggled to let out a dim whisper.

He coughed up a weak laugh. "You think you know everything, all of you. You have no idea."

"How can it be too late? He's still alive. Try! Please, someone, try!" Scarlett spoke for the first time in the Lyceum. In spite of everything she had been through, her spirit hadn't been defeated.

When I heard her voice, I felt compelled to look at her. She was as fierce as ever. There was fear, but not for herself. She held my gaze in the way she always had, but this time, I could barely see her usual warmth beneath all the pain and pity.

She was holding on to Evan's arm. She trusted him.

"There is nothing we can do." Edmeer's tone was earnest, but Scarlett ignored him. Instead, she looked at me. I shook my head, urging her to accept Dru's fate, but she refused. She ran to Dru, clutching a knife in one hand.

I tried to jump to Scarlett, but the heavy wind pushed me back down. By the time I got to her, she'd already slit her wrist and held it over to Dru, letting her blood drip on him. I ripped some material from my clothes to tie on her wound. Then I pulled her in my arms and buried my face on her shoulder—no longer caring what the Supreme Eltors would make of it. "You're more reckless than I am. Your blood won't work. It has to be from an Arca. An Eltor."

"I had to try something. That's Dru, and he's dying. Everyone is just letting him die." Tears streamed down Scarlett's face.

"A clever move, Spark, giving her a knife. Risky but clever," Dru murmured, his voice faint and hoarse.

"Are you still so keen on killing someone who is willing to sacrifice her life to save an Empyr?" Evan didn't direct his question to anyone in particular, but it rendered every Supreme Eltor thoughtful for a few seconds. Everyone was taken aback, and even Kalista was silent.

"A human tries to save my life, and an Astra and a Spark are determined to protect hers. Why? What is so precious about the life you know, you're so afraid to let it go? Limits. Systems. Rules. Restrictions. Sins. You have absolutely nothing. You're fighting so hard just to feel a drop of that illusive happiness, and I'm bathing in it. I'm free." Dru's face had deteriorated to the point that he struggled to speak. Yet, his words were sharp.

He might be right. The free will we thought we had might be nothing more than an illusion, but so was his elation. I felt the deception of its poison, but the love I had for Scarlett was stronger. Real.

I held Scarlett tighter in my embrace as we witnessed Dru's body disintegrate until there was nothing left but his emerald Exir, ultimately shattering into a multitude of sparks. Scarlett was the only one weeping, but everyone's sorrow was evident. Only when the last flicker of Dru's Exir had been extinguished did someone dare to speak.

It was Harper who broke the silence. "We have lost one Eltor. We can't afford to lose another. Everything we're doing is to protect you, Petyr. We're not your enemy."

I felt the sincerity of Harper's judicious statement, but I wasn't willing to compromise. "I know, but I won't pay the price of that protection, not with Scarlett's life."

"One day, it will be too much to resist," Oswald stated, not as a warning but a fact.

"Not if he keeps his distance," Evan interjected. His voice was louder than everyone else's, perhaps trying to ensure he was heard in a place where no Spark had ever been acknowledged before. He, too, wasn't as confident as he would like to appear in front of the Supreme Eltors.

No one responded to Evan's words, at least not directly. When Kalista spoke, she addressed the other Supreme Eltors, without glancing at the Spark's direction. Her voice was still stern, but somewhat less hostile. "She knows too much about us."

"Then she will have to forget. If we allow her to live, we can't allow her to remember," Rex declared through his enduring impassive veneer.

"No," I objected, regaining the control in my voice. Dru was right. I might have been able to resist the *Forbidden* several times, but I wasn't free. I knew my strength, and I knew my worth. It was time to make the Supreme Eltors realize the power they had over me was just as much of an illusion as the free will I thought I had. I caught a faint smile on Evan's face before I continued, "I won't be bound by your rules. You may predict, but you don't get to decide my fate. I won't stay away from her. She won't die, and she won't forget—"

"I want to forget." Scarlett's voice was so familiar, yet I resented the words it formed. The satisfied smile on Evan's face grew more visible. This was exactly what he wanted. His motivation was another in the long line of questions I couldn't answer.

"I have put you through so much pain, and I have betrayed your trust because of my own fears. Asking for your forgiveness is already too much. I don't expect you to accept me. You know what I'm capable of, but I promise, I don't know how else to make you believe, but I promise, I will never let any harm come to you—"

She didn't wait for me to finish before she kissed me, gentle and earnest, relishing every pulse of a moment. When she pulled away, I knew her mind hadn't changed.

"I love you," she whispered, "I love you so much, and I don't care what you are. I want nothing more than to be with you, forever. But every second you're with me, you're always at risk. I can't be with you knowing I could turn you into"—she closed her eyes for a few seconds, unable to bring herself to describe Dru's decaying body—"into something that would eradicate everything that you are."

After everything she had seen and heard, she should be appalled. She should resent me. Instead, she tried to protect me. Even now, she still managed to surprise me.

"I can't. Please," I pleaded.

"I won't be able to stay away if I remember you."

I didn't respond. I had to respect her decision. It made sense. She would be safer away from me, and she would be free from all the pain I had and would cause her. Still, I couldn't find the voice to say yes. I held her in my arms until I heard Evan's voice. "As it happens, I have a spare potion in my pocket."

EPILOGUE

"This is Celestria," I whispered.

Scarlett and I stood on the pinnacle of my shelter, above the sky of Empyrian, in the Astran region. Here, our shelters were larger than those in the Santrum. Each had a glow with specific shades and tones reflecting the strength of its Owner's Exir.

I hadn't let Scarlett go from my grasp since the moment we left the Lyceum. Even now, as we stood side by side, gazing at the cosmos above and the world below, I kept her hand locked with mine.

Scarlett's eyes wandered in awe at the vast magnificence of the planetary bodies and galaxies above. "Can you go to all of those planets?"

"Not all. There are certain places that require a much stronger Exir than I have right now." I felt a sense of ease in admitting a weakness. I knew it was too late to matter, but a part of me was still trying to find connections with Scarlett. I wanted her to see my abilities had limits. There were places I, too, wasn't able to reach.

"What do you do on the ones you can reach?"

The eagerness in her eyes told me she was expecting a description of my journey in the cosmos. I knew she wanted more in my response, but all I could manage was a straightforward answer. "Learn."

She exhaled a soft chuckle. "Trust you to make something that looks incredibly exciting sound tedious."

I could tell her so much about my experiences in the centuries I traveled the different places above, but none of it mattered. I spent my entire existence believing that exploring these places and gaining knowledge was my main purpose. I was a mere vessel that wasted so much time working to ensure the Exir inside me grew stronger, chained in the illusion that this was what I wanted. Never truly alive, not until I met Scarlett. When I didn't respond with more than a dim smile, her own smile seemed to have faded into the anxiety she'd been trying to conceal. "How long will it take for the potion to erase you from my memory?"

I held her hand tighter. I needed her warmth to propel enough strength that would enable me to answer the question I dreaded. I filled my lungs with air before I spoke, hoping the wind would carry the weight of each word. "It will start when you fall asleep. It will be done when you wake up." We were silent for a while after that.

Her legs trembled slightly, either from exhaustion or fear—or both. Still silent, I sat down and guided her to rest her head on my lap. My hand glided through her disheveled curls. Every tangle was a bitter reminder of the formidable journey I had led her to. I traced the edges of her face, willing my fingers to never forget the shape, to remember how her skin felt against mine.

My heart began to sink as her eyes closed for a few seconds. When she finally opened them and caught the agony on my face, she pressed a hand on my arm. A reassurance that she was still with me. "Evan helped us, you know. They didn't catch us. He asked me if I wanted to help you, and we found them." Her breathing was slow as she spoke, but each syllable was carried by forced vitality. She seemed to be exerting a considerable amount of effort to fight the fatigue, to delay the sleep.

"He placed a knife in your hand, knowing full well you'd use it." I cringed at the memory of the blood she had willingly spilled. "He placed you within reach of the

Supreme Eltors, who had every intention of taking your life." My words were laced with shame. I had done the very same the moment I told her what I was.

"But he helped dissuade the Supreme Eltors from"—she hesitated—"killing me."

"I don't trust him." I wanted her to hear the warning in my tone, but a part of me knew it didn't matter. When she woke from her sleep, she wouldn't remember anything about my world, not him, not me.

"I think I do." I felt a sting at hearing the confirmation, but I couldn't blame her. Evan made her understand the dreadful truths I hadn't the strength to, and he had a plan, one that was far superior to mine. He saved her when I couldn't. He didn't let her down, and I'd done nothing but just that. I couldn't bring myself to contradict Scarlett's decision, but I couldn't agree with her either. When it came to Evan, for now, I had nothing more to say.

We fell silent once again, but as every blink of her eyes lingered longer than the previous, I urged myself to speak. "I will never leave you. Even if you don't remember me, I will always be there to make sure you're safe."

She shook her head. "It will only hurt you to see me."

"It will hurt me more not to." I wanted to say more. I wanted to explain why it was necessary for me to be close to her, even after she had forgotten me. I wanted to convince her. But a sharp echo, stuck in my chest, restrained my voice.

Once again, we fell into the unkind depth of silence.

"What will happen when I wake up?" Scarlett broke the silence this time.

"You'll be in your own bed, opening your eyes to a typical day. Your parents and everyone else will also forget me. The others are working on it as we speak. I will take you back myself. When you wake up, all the pain I've caused you would have faded away." I forced myself to smile, to try to find comfort in knowing she would also forget the pain.

She took my hand and placed it on her chest. "I didn't choose to forget because I was hurt. I'd do it all again. The love I feel for you is not something that can be erased. I believe that." She kissed my hand and let her eyelids fall. She no longer fought to open her eyes as she uttered her final words. "Even if I forget your face, I will never stop loving you."

"I can't give up. I'm sorry. I love you too much to let you go," I whispered when I was sure she had fallen asleep. I lifted her into my arms, unwilling to take her home, unwilling to let her go. I'd have to break another promise.

CPSIA information can be obtained at www.ICGtesting.com
Printed in the USA
BVOW02s1740190516

448775BV00002B/2/P